TOBIAS JONES

White Death

ff

faber and faber

First published in 2011
by Faber and Faber Limited
Bloomsbury House,
74–77 Great Russell Street,
London WC1B 3DA
This paperback edition first published in 2012

Typeset by RefineCatch Limited, Bungay, Suffolk
Printed in England by CPI Group (UK) Ltd, Croydon CR0 4YY

A CIP record for this book
is available from the British Library

ISBN 978-0-571-23714-2

2 4 6 8 10 9 7 5 3 1

For Jonathan and Suzi Herbert

It was just after eight o'clock when the phone started trilling impatiently. I had been awake for hours, leaving the lights off so I could watch the dawn turn the cupolas orange and pink. I enjoyed the silence of the sleeping city, the absence of all the usual noise of shouting and cars. In the last two hours my peace had slowly ebbed away: the stars had sunk back into the sky and the traffic had started to build up outside my window. Then the phone started its ugly electronic prod and I knew the day had begun.

'Pronto,' I said.

'Castagnetti?' asked an impatient voice.

'That's me.'

'You're the private detective, right?'

'Sort of.' I try to avoid the term because it makes people think in stereotypes. 'I offer clarity in criminal cases,' I said slowly.

'I've a job for you.'

'And you are?'

He said his name was Pino Bragantini, said it slowly like it was the kind of name that people normally recognised. I had never heard of him.

'What's the job?'

'I'll tell you in person if you don't mind. Face to face.'

'Fair enough. Where are you?'

I

He gave me his address. He said it was some factory to the south of the city. Said he wanted to see me there immediately if that were possible. I told him it was.

I hung up and looked out of the window. It was the beginning of one of those blissful spring days without a cloud. The sky was infinite blue and the sun winked off windscreens and sunglasses. There was a gentle wind combing the city, hurrying scontrini across the cobbles and ruffling the rabbit-skin cuffs of people's coats.

I twisted apart the macchinetta and filled it with water, scooped in some coffee and twisted it back together. I put it on the gas and went to have my weekly shave. I looked at myself in the mirror: my short hair was going grey at the temples and as I scraped the blade across my face I noticed how the stubble in the sink looked like salt and pepper. More salt than pepper. I would be forty in a couple of years' time and here I was, still living in a provincial city not even knowing what to call my job.

By the time I got back to the kitchen, the coffee was spluttering across the hob, the top of the macchinetta bouncing up and down as the brown liquid spat in all directions. I drank it quickly and got dressed.

Outside the traffic was static. It was the normal rush-hour standstill. I decided to walk to the factory since it was only just the other side of the city. It wouldn't take long, even allowing for my gammy ankle. Someone had taken objection to me getting my foot in the door a few years back and it has never been right since. Doctors keep saying I need to exercise it but every time my left heel leaves the ground I feel the area around my tendon twinge. It's not an acute pain, but I'm always aware of it. When it's quiet I can even hear it crackling like a peal of distant fireworks. And when it's cold or damp, or I've been driving for too long, the whole thing seizes up completely and the only way I can walk is to drag it along behind me. And that brings two things I never want: attention and sympathy. People stare or smile like they're sorry for me.

So I limped up towards the factory, amazed at how bedraggled our beautiful city appeared. It had begun to contract. Shops were closing down, windows were being covered with large red letters at oblique angles: 'vendita totale'. Exotic clothes and mighty mannequins had been replaced by whitewashed glass and hopeless, handwritten notes: 'to let'. It was like the city had a puncture and was losing air all the time. No amount of pumping or repair seemed to make any difference.

The crisis had been going on for a few years now and it had hit this city hard. I looked at people's faces and they seemed desperate. Short of money and patience. They seemed more pallid, as if they couldn't afford the skiing or even the tanning clinics any more. The place felt less glamorous, less flashy all of a sudden. Before, people had spent thousands just to keep up, to look right, to fit in and feel good. Now there was nothing to keep up with, nothing to fit into. All the masks and costumes of the carnival had been put away, sold off, and we were left with the dull reality of our dull selves. No feathers, no fancy dress, only the struggle for survival.

I got to the factory an hour later. It was a beautiful spot. Cypresses and poplars creating elegant avenues, the gurgle of the nearby river. It felt like an oasis in the urban jungle. The factory itself looked unusually august, as if it had been there for at least the last hundred years.

I walked in the front door and saw a receptionist. She was young and dark-skinned, with spray-on clothes over nice curves. As I got closer I realised she was wearing too much perfume. She smelt like the inside of a taxi with too many magic trees.

'I'm here to see Bragantini,' I said.

'And you are?'

'Castagnetti.'

She picked up the phone and told him I was here. He came out a few minutes later: a shortish man, mid-fifties, bald head with a grey halo of hair and a bushy grey moustache that covered his mouth. He dressed like someone used to hiding behind elegance: smart suit, serious tie, sober shoes. I noticed a chunky watch as we shook hands. He took me into his office and showed me to a chair.

'Thank you for coming,' he said.

'Thank you for calling. How can I help?'

'I've got a problem.'

I nodded.

'I've been the victim of an arson attack.'

I looked at him. No burns. 'Where?'

'My car. Last night. Windows smashed, petrol poured in. By the time I got here this morning my Audi was a wreck.'

'What kind of Audi?'

'An A4 Saloon.'

'Nice sled.'

'It was,' he said regretfully. He stared into space in memory of his car.

4

'What time did you get here this morning?' I asked.

'Seven. I always start early. Have to be here that early just to tackle the paperwork. I never have time during the day.'

'And what is this place?'

'The factory?' He looked up, surprised that I didn't know. 'We produce bottles. And bottle tops.'

'Bottles?'

'And bottling machinery.'

'Many rivals?'

'Most of the city. Every other businessman around these parts is into something similar. That's our distretto. Some cities specialise in sofas or tiles or automobiles. Our speciality is food engineering.'

I nodded as if impressed. 'And the car? You got insurance?'

'Sure, but that's not the point.'

'What is the point?'

'Someone's targeting me, deliberately setting fire to my property.'

'How do you know it wasn't just some hooligan trying to keep himself warm at night?'

He shook his head impatiently. 'Look where we are. No one comes up this way, day or night. This isn't the kind of place you just chance upon. Someone's trying to intimidate me and I want to know who and why.'

He didn't seem like the sort of man to suffer intimidation. His stare was intense and it pinned me to the chair.

'Let's start with who,' I said. 'Any ideas?'

'Mah!' he said impatiently. 'I've had to lay off a few workers recently. What with the crisis. They weren't happy, I suppose, but I can't see them ever pulling a stunt like this.'

'I'll need their names and addresses.'

He nodded curtly.

'Have you,' I paused, not sure how to say it, 'have you made anyone jealous recently?'

'What does that mean?'

'It means', I gave up on delicacy, 'have you been screwing another man's wife?'

He ran his thumb and forefinger down each side of his moustache like he was thinking about it.

'I'll need that name and address too.'

'I didn't hire you to delve into my private life.'

'You haven't hired me yet. And if you do, I'll delve wherever I want.'

'There's only one,' he looked up at me, talking quietly, 'and her husband doesn't know.'

'Who knows who knows?' I said. 'People have a sixth sense when they start sprouting horns.'

He stared at me. 'I need discretion.'

'And I'll need those names.'

He nodded, looking at me with a tilted head like he disliked me already. He leant forward and pressed a button on his desk.

'Nunzia, bring in the addresses of all the employees we let go in the autumn.'

He hung up and stared at me again. 'How much?'

I told him, and he wrote it down, whistling like he thought I was a rip-off.

'Expenses on top,' I said.

He looked at me and forced a laugh.

The receptionist came in with a few sheets of paper.

'Could you write your address on here too?' he asked her.

She nodded. 'Sì dottore.' She went round beside him and scribbled on the paper.

'Thank you.'

She turned round to go and Bragantini caught my eye.

'She your squeeze?' I said as the door closed behind her.

'Her name's Nunzia Di Michele. Her address is here.' He took out a pen and I saw his hand circling something on the pages. He passed the paper across to me. There were a few addresses across the city and the receptionist's handwritten one.

'Discretion,' he said.

I nodded. 'Any rival particularly competitive, got a grudge, anything like that?'

'All of them.'

'And are they likely to pull a stunt like this?'

He stared at his desk, narrowing his eyes. 'I doubt it. What would they gain from burning my car?'

'Give me the names anyway.'

I passed him back the paper and he picked up a pen and started writing on the back of the list of addresses.

'You got security?'

He shrugged like he didn't know what that meant. 'I lock up. I set the alarm.'

'No CCTV?'

He shook his head.

'Dogs?'

Same again.

'You might want to think about stepping things up, maybe get a night porter, someone to keep an eye out.'

'I thought that's what I was employing you for.'

'I'll come by when I can,' I said. 'But I'm not a security guard. Get someone on it. Someone who can watch out for you when you're not around.'

He twisted his head like he didn't like the mounting costs.

'You want to show me the car?' I said, trying to take his mind off it.

He nodded in silence and stood up. He passed me the list of addresses as he led the way out of the room. 'Back in five minutes,' he said to the receptionist. I looked at her and peered over her desk. There was a photograph of a young man next to her computer screen who I assumed was her husband.

Bragantini led me across to the car park. I could smell the car even before I could see it. It was little more than a burnt-out box. Much of the metal was black and flaky. It looked like an automobile skeleton, with the gear stick and steering wheel stripped of all flesh. Bragantini stared at it and shook his head.

'This happened last night?'

He nodded.

'You always leave your car at work overnight?'

'Not always, but I only live over there.' He bounced his chin in the direction of a block of flats through the trees. 'I spend so much time in the car during the day that come the evening I'm happy to have a short walk home.'

'And why not call the police?'

He rocked his head backwards and rolled his eyes. 'You know the answer to that. They haven't got the time or resources to dedicate to this kind of case. They give a very good impression of not even caring.'

'But you've reported it?'

'I will,' he said unconvincingly. 'But the only reason I would even do that is for insurance purposes. I don't expect them to dedicate any more time to this than it takes to fill in a form.'

'Which insurance company are you with?'

'Gruppo Sicurezza.'

I looked at him again and wondered why he was even wasting money on me. He would get reimbursed for the cost of the car, so it wasn't as if he had had anything stolen as such. He must have known that I would get no further than the usual authorities, and would just cost him a few thousand on top.

'Why did you call me in?' I asked. 'If it was a hooligan having his fun, it's hardly worth hiring a private.'

'You don't want the job?'

I threw my palms in the air. 'I'm happy for any work I can get, but I like to know why I'm getting it. It doesn't seem to make much sense.'

He grunted, and looked behind me, right and left. 'This car park is half full most nights.' He took a step towards me to underline what he was saying. 'There are probably about a dozen company cars here every night. Now if one of those had been torched I might be able to ignore it. But of those dozen cars they deliberately went for my personal one.' He suddenly looked at me and nodded. 'That makes me think whoever did this wasn't some idiot arsonist, but someone who was trying to send a direct message to me. I want to know what that message is, and who sent it.'

It made more sense like that. I nodded and shook his hand.

I promised to do what I could. He walked back inside and I turned to examine the burnt-out car. I knelt down and looked underneath. I peered inside. There was nothing to go on. I wandered over towards the river and watched it for a minute or two: there was a rusty can of Coke, the red and white only just visible below the blanket of algae. There was a bike lock down there, a few shredded plastic bags hanging onto bushes, the wide, transparent triangle of a sandwich wrapper bouncing on the plaited waters towards the open seas.

I walked off, reading the list of addresses as I went. I still thought it likely that some random hooligan had found a smart car and burnt it for fun. It was probably just chance they had burnt Bragantini's. Or maybe they had gone for it because it was clearly the smartest.

Either way I wasn't exactly excited about it. Getting an arson case is like being asked to work out who's sprayed a slogan on your wall in the middle of the night. The chances of catching the culprit are very small. And even if you do, it's hardly high-end work. Most of the arson cases I had worked on were insurance jobs. People bored of their unprofitable businesses and cumbersome assets that no one wanted to buy, so they torched the lot. Except this time that didn't look likely. Bragantini wouldn't have hired me if it had been him who poured petrol all over his wheels.

Which left me with disgruntled employees taking revenge. I looked at their addresses on the sheets of paper. They were in different parts of the city, so I planned a route from one to the other, wishing I had brought the car after all.

It took me most of the morning to cross them off the list of suspects. I pretended to be from social services, checking up on the well-being of people who found themselves out of work. One came out with the old line that it was the best thing that had ever happened to him. Said he had been longing to leave the company for years, and that he could now finally follow his dream. Which meant, as far as I could work out from the thick odour of his front room, sitting at home and smoking spliffs.

The next one had moved back to Napoli months ago and his flat-mates hadn't seen him since. They didn't have a forwarding address for him, but they gave me his old mobile number. I called him up and left a message.

And the third one had, according to his wife, been working at another factory for the last few months.

I phoned one of the men Bragantini had said was a business rival. I pretended to be from Bragantini's insurance company, checking up all leads in an arson case. The secretary offered to make an appointment for next week, so I hung up and went round in person. I flashed my badge and waited for him to get back from lunch.

'Insurance investigator, eh?' he said cheerily when his secretary introduced us.

I told him about the fire at Bragantini's and he smiled. 'And he thinks I did it?'

'I'm talking to everyone in the same line as him,' I said curtly.

'Then you've got a long day. There are hundreds of us in this line.'

'All bottling?'

'Bottling, canning, tinning. That sort of thing. "Culinary engineering".' He smiled at the grandiose sound of the term.

I spoke to him for a quarter of an hour. He told me where he was the previous night and gave me the addresses of the friends he had been with. He seemed amused rather than disconcerted by the whole thing, and I crossed him off the list as well. One by one I eliminated the other rivals, the unlikely arsonists who had decent alibis and no motive.

I went back home to get my car. It was late afternoon by then and I parked outside the receptionist's address on a small street which ran off the Via Emilia. I walked up to the intercom and saw the usual panel of two dozen names. I found Nunzia Di Michele's name and, next to hers, what I assumed was her husband's: Michelotti. I sat in the car for an hour, waiting for someone to come out. Eventually a young man emerged who looked dark, with a thin face and a thin mouth like the photo on the receptionist's desk. I fired up the car and followed him. He drove for a mile out of town, stopping at a roadside bar. I waited for him to walk in before getting out and following him inside.

The bar was the usual dark hole, most of the light coming from a small TV sitting on a black metal plate in the corner. There were a few posters of B movies from twenty years ago and a pennant of the city's football team. I saw a pine tree of Chupa lollies by the cash till and a large Gaggia coffee machine. There were folded newspapers on wobbly, circular tables and old chairs with faded floral seats complete with cigarette burns and yellowing chewing gum in the corners. There was a ridgeback dog in there, too energetic for the claustrophobic bar. It came round panting and licking, knocking tables with its chest and chin and spilling drinks onto people's laps which it then tried to lick. It was the kind of place that was never closed and never cleaned, one of those unfashionable holes in the suburbs where people went just because it was there.

The husband was sitting on a barstool drinking a beer. I sat next to him and ordered the usual malvasia. The barman looked like his dog and had the same breath. He was talking away, telling anyone who would listen why the Caprazucca bridge, the 'goat-pumpkin' bridge, had such a daft name.

'It was built by a man called Capri Succhi and over the years it became, in the popular imagination, Caprazucca.'

'That's bull,' said another man at the bar. 'Everyone thinks that but it's not true.' The barman was offended, but stood there listening to the new expert. 'It used to be called the bridge of Donna Egidia, but it was wooden and rotting. So they built a new one. This was some time in the thirteenth century.'

'Allora?' the barman said impatiently, wanting to put his rival back in his place.

'In the fifteenth century some constable called Antonio da Godano was the officer on the bridge and you know what his nickname was?'

'Goat-pumpkin?' the barman said.

The man looked at us seriously. 'You got it. Capra-zucca.'

'What kind of nickname is that?' I asked. Goat-pumpkin sounded like a daft nickname to me.

'It's an old way to say piggy-back. "Cravasu'cca". Sounds like "capra-zucca" you see? The constable's nickname was piggy-back, and since piggy-back was there, guarding the bridge and doubtless charging people to use it, the bridge got his nickname too.'

'Why would a constable get such an idiotic nickname?' asked the husband, wanting to point out the old man's ignorance.

'That's lost in the mists of time,' said the man, narrowing his eyes and focusing on the wall behind the bar as if he had said something very profound. 'But I have a few theories . . .'

He was waiting for us to beg him to spill, so I threw my chin in the air, which was the only cue he needed.

'He was a soldier. He probably saw action, since back then every town and village was at war with its neighbour. It may be that he earned his nickname by rescuing his comrades and carrying them piggy-back.'

'Maybe he was just a hunchback,' the barman said.

'We get the idea,' I said more impatiently than I intended. I wanted to wrap things up and get the husband alone. 'Another malvasia.'

'Right away.'

The barman turned his back to go to the fridge. The husband and I caught each other's eyes and smiled.

'Fucking Goat-pumpkin,' he said under his breath.

We sat there for a while, watching the barman uncork a new bottle. The conversation reminded me what a strange country this was. Everywhere the past seems to dwarf the present. The first lesson you learn in this city is that you can never match the majesty of our ancestors: those proud palazzi and gold-plated libraries and frescoed churches will never be bettered. The most you can hope for is to be allowed inside them or, failing that, become an erudite drunk. For fifteen hundred years this peninsula has lived in the shadow of the greatest empire known to man. And to have your glory behind you is a sure way to become fatalistic and decadent. It means that all learning faces backwards rather than forwards. We feel like we're living in the ruins and debris of a glorious history and can only sit and wonder why we arrived too late. It's the same as my line of work. I'm only ever called when something's already happened, when all the action is in the past . . . and I limp along pessimistically, trying to understand what went on by looking at the ruins and the ruined lives.

I looked over at the TV. As usual there were girls in bikinis doing provocative dances in front of old male presenters with unnaturally black hair.

'Look at them,' I said, staring at the TV.

'I'm looking, I'm looking,' the husband laughed.

'What do you think they have to do to get on television?' I asked.

'Eh beh!' He laughed again. 'I'm sure there are quite a few casting sessions.'

We watched the girls for a couple of minutes. They were smiling stupidly at the camera, cavorting around in their red, sequined outfits.

'You married?' I asked.

'Yeah, I'm married.'

'Lucky man.'

He turned round to look at me and smiled, nodding his head towards the TV screen. 'She doesn't look much like them though.'

I was waiting for the first hint of misogyny, a revelation of hatred for his wife and for his marriage. But he surprised me. He told me how they had met and married, where they lived and what they wanted to do with their lives. They didn't have any children yet, he said, but they would once they had saved enough money to buy a small flat. He seemed like a devoted husband, entirely ignorant about what his wife was up to. No man who knew he had been cuckolded would have spoken about their dreams like that. I wished him luck, downed the rest of my drink and walked out. Another potential arsonist in the clear.

I got back to my little monolocale and sat in darkness. I could hear the roar of mopeds going past outside and from the flat below I got the incessant stupidity of some TV quiz show. The audience laughter and applause sounded even more canned when coming up through the floor. I sat there, on the one chair in the one-room flat, feeling defeated. I had wasted a day. I had lied to everyone I had met, pretending to be from social services, or from an insurance company. I had pretended to be a barfly. I felt like a fraud without a lead. Everything seemed pointless.

I was falling asleep in the chair when the phone went. I picked it up and put it to my ear. Before I could say anything I heard that same impatient voice. 'Castagnetti?'

'Who's this?'

'Bragantini.'

'Nothing to report yet,' I said quickly, defensively.

'Yeah, well I have. I just got a call. The kind of caller who doesn't leave a name.'

'And?'

'They said it was time for me to think about the safety of my workers and my family. He mentioned the names of my children. Said there was too much criminality in the city for a factory like mine to be safe. Said it would be better for my peace of mind to move out to the sticks, that it wasn't safe around this area any more.'

'Not much veil to that threat. What did you say?'

'I told him to go back to his whoring mother.'

'Nice. When was this?'

'Just now.' The guy sounded like he was still shaking with rage. 'They called me at home.'

I sat up and tried to concentrate.

'I'm ex-directory,' he said.

'Makes the threat more threatening.'

'But no one knows my home number. Everyone uses my mobile.'

I asked him for both numbers and wrote them down. 'I'll come round,' I said.

He hung up without saying anything.

I was up there a quarter of an hour later. His wife was fussing around in her dressing gown, trying to calm her husband down. He introduced us and we shook hands. She was a tall, good-looking woman whose face suggested she had spent too many years worrying about life. Either that or she was a heavy smoker: lines were etched across her face, but they made her somehow more attractive, more human.

Bragantini took me into his study and poured two generous slugs of whiskey.

'Sit down,' he ordered. He remained standing, still too jittery to sit. He was shaking his head violently, the way people do when they're trying to get water out of an ear.

'The caller,' I said. 'It was a man, I assume?'

He nodded.

'Accent?'

He shrugged. 'Usual. Nothing special about it.'

'Would you recognise it again?'

He threw his hands in the air in impatience. I brought him up to date with what I had done all day and he seemed as unimpressed as I was.

'Did you think about security?' I asked.

'I'll get on to it tomorrow.'

'File a report with the authorities as well. It's always good to have something like this logged in case it ever comes to court. Most crime is incremental. Domestic violence might end in murder but it usually starts with a flick of the ear, you with me?'

He nodded. 'You know what this is about? Someone wants to buy me out and setting my car alight is how they open negotiations.'

'If they call again,' I said, so he understood, 'tell them you want to negotiate. Set up a meeting.'

'I'm not selling,' he said defiantly.

'I know,' I said slowly, 'but they don't need to know that.'

He grunted in irritation. He was a determined sort, the kind of man to become more stubborn in the face of thugs and their threats. He wasn't particularly endearing: he was hard-nosed and probably hard-hearted. He spoke with the caps lock on and cheated on his wife. But there was something about him I admired. He was unflinching, courageous in an aggressive sort of way. And I was secretly pleased at what had happened. What had appeared a dead-end case of vandalism had suddenly got a lot more interesting.

'We need them out in the open,' I said. 'They've shown

their hand. We just need them to show their face. If they think you're really going to sell, they'll come out sooner or later. Or at least, they'll send someone out.'

He didn't like the idea of even pretending to sell, but he could see the point.

We held each other's stares for a second like we were shaking hands. I got up to go, thanking him for the drink.

'I'm counting on you, Castagnetti,' he shouted at my back as I walked over the gravel drive towards my car. I waved a hand over my shoulder.

I was too wired when I got home to go to sleep. I sat in the car thinking about the amount of money his factory would be worth if it were converted to flats. They would probably keep the nice, nineteenth-century façade, sand-blast off the ochre lichen and gut the rest. Make it into some kind of luxury living complex, as swanky and soulless as all the others. It would be worth a fortune.

It was past midnight now. I drove out to the city's main fire station. It was in a large warehouse on the outskirts of town. A line of rectangular, red engines were lined up ready for the next call. To the side was an office shaped like a cube of thin aluminium.

The door was open but there was no one around. I walked in and saw in the light from the street that the walls were covered with posters advising the public to fit smoke alarms and stock up on fire blankets and extinguishers. There was a calendar on the wall with photographs of fire stations around the peninsula. They all looked exactly the same, only the backdrop was different: mountains, seaside, concrete.

'Hello?' I shouted. 'Anyone around?'

There was no reply. I opened a side door and saw a corridor of lockers on one side and doors on the other. Above the corridor was a balcony with more doors.

'Anyone around?' I shouted again as I walked upstairs. There had to be someone because they always kept a couple of people at the station on stand-by. I walked down the corridor, knocking on doors, not waiting for a reply but knocking hard and moving on to the next one.

'What's going on?' a voice said behind me.

I turned round and saw a man in a tracksuit. He was taller than me and had a jawline as wide as my shoulders.

I held out a card for him. He took it and looked down at me.

'You're an investigator?'

'You can read then?'

'Very funny. What are you doing sneaking around here at night?'

'I'm not sneaking. The door was open.'

'What do you want?' he said, losing patience.

I told him about the burnt-out car. He said he had heard about it. Said it happened every now and again. Said that conviction rates were in single figures, if not fractions.

'Why do they do it?' I asked.

He shrugged. 'I could tell you if we ever caught them. My guess is a combination of the usual. Insurance job. Jealous spouse. Working-class hero with a chip on their shoulder. The anarchist who doesn't believe in the system. The eco-warrior who doesn't believe in the internal combustion engine. Or, most likely, some loser who likes to watch flames, to see the chaos they can create just by striking a match. It gives them a sense of power, of manipulating events, of being a creator of sorts.'

'You got records of all car fires?'

He laughed. 'We got records for everything. You can't flush a toilet here without filling in the right piece of paperwork. We got records, all right.'

'Open to the public?'

He shook his head. 'The office is locked until tomorrow.'

People are always saying to me that they can't give out information. Which normally means they'll happily sell it. I've never met anyone who believes more in privacy than in money. Open your wallet and they normally open their mouth. I held out a fifty.

He looked at me with disgust. 'Put it away,' he said with authority.

I put the note away and looked at the jawline. 'I'm just trying to save lives, the same as you,' I said.

'That so?' he said with sarcasm.

'I'll make an official request in the morning.'

'You do that.'

He stood at the door to his room, watching me slink down the stairs like a naughty child. I didn't like the humiliation, but I was pleased that my jaundiced world view wasn't entirely correct. There were people who didn't take cash in the middle of the night. There were people who wouldn't do anything for a bit of easy money. It didn't help me, but it cheered me up a little.

I woke up early the next morning and went straight back to the fire station. It took a fair amount of bluster to get what I wanted. The woman on the front desk made a point of being unhelpful and the man with the jawline wasn't around. Eventually I got to speak to some public liaison person who gave me a list of car fires in the last two years. There were sixteen in total. I couldn't take all the documentation with me, so I made a generous donation to the retired firemen's fund and got the charmer on the front desk to make photocopies.

I went from one address to the next. Most of them were out, or had moved away, so I wasted the morning limping from one place to the next just to ring a doorbell a couple of times. It was raining heavily and within an hour my clothes were stuck to my back and I was bored.

To those who were in, I told the truth: that I was looking into all car fires in the last two years to try and establish some sort of pattern. They came out with their own theories, used my appearance as an excuse to get an old grudge off their chest. Out of politeness I wrote down names they mentioned – former boyfriends, or business partners, or local eccentrics – and promised to follow up the leads. They seemed surprised that anyone would still be interested in their case because no one had seemed particularly interested when it had happened.

They told me what new car they had bought as a replacement, told me in detail about how it was better, or worse, than the one they had had before. I took down the names of their insurance companies, just in case.

I had been to about a dozen addresses when something interesting came up. I had been looking for a man called Carlo Lombardi, a prosciutto merchant whose Volvo had been charcoaled a year ago. The address I had for him was a prosciuttificio half a mile to the north. It wasn't a particularly pleasant area: hemmed in by the railway, the ring road and the motorway. I decided to drive there since it was so out of the way and it was still raining heavily. I went up and down the road twice without seeing the place. Normally a prosciuttificio has its prices on display outside, large numbers describing weights and the length of stagionatura. They normally have a forecourt where customers can park to pick up their ham wholesale, get a whole leg instead of a few wafers of the stuff.

It was supposed to be number 17, but in the hundred-metre stretch between 15 and 19, all I could see was chaos. Steel straws stuck out of square concrete pillars. The building was a shell of thick grey lines. It was entirely hollow but for a concrete staircase which ran from one non-floor to the next. Red and blue flexi tubes protruded from windows. Above, two cranes moved slowly like the arms of a clock which had lost their centre. There was the constant noise of banging, only offset by the booming voices of the workers: parolacce and laughter, random shouts and snatches of famous songs. The place smelt of wet sand.

I got out of the car and walked up to the site. Facing the

road was a large white sign detailing the construction firm, the engineer, the architect and the timescale for the building. The official rubbish. I took the phone out of my pocket and snapped a shot. I looked at the result and checked I could read the names. The main one was easy. It was written in large letters at the top: Masi Costruzioni.

I walked towards a portakabin a few metres from the pavement. It had Masi flags flying from each corner. I knocked on the door.

'Avanti,' someone shouted from inside.

I opened the door and saw a man at a desk. 'You're the first person who has ever knocked on that door.' He laughed, his earlobes wobbling as he bounced. 'Who are you?'

'I was just passing,' I said, faking timidity, 'and wondered . . . are there still flats for sale?'

'I've no idea. Not my role.'

'Isn't this the ufficio vendite?'

'No, I'm just the foreman. Trying to make sure work gets done on time.'

'Does it?'

'What?'

'Get done on time?'

'Depends how often I'm distracted.' He looked at me over his half-moon glasses. His face was all ears and nose. It was a sad face, the face of someone who was downtrodden but loyal and strangely shrewd. The face of someone who had been bullied, but who had cut a deal with the bullies.

'It says on the board the flats will be ready for consegna at the end of the summer.'

'It will have to be a very long summer,' he laughed.

24

'How long you been on it?'

'Since last autumn.'

'Wasn't this where the old prosciuttificio used to be? What was it called? Lombardozzi or something?'

He shrugged. 'Wouldn't know.'

'So where's the ufficio vendite?'

'In the centro. Sales are being handled by some agency.'

'Any idea who?'

He grunted, growing bored of the disturbance. He stood up and went over to a board and tilted his head backwards so he was looking through his glasses. 'Casa dei Sogni it's called.'

The phone started ringing. 'Scusi,' he said and picked it up.

I held up a palm by way of goodbye and walked out. I drove a few blocks and parked outside a bar. Bar staff are the next best thing to parish priests when it comes to street-level intelligence. No one knows the territory like them. They hear all the gossip and complaints and grievances.

There was a petite woman serving. 'What can I get you?' she asked.

'Malvasia.'

She poured it like she was watering a plant, sloshing it out so fast that the glass moved towards me as it filled up. Fizzing drops fell onto the counter.

I raised the glass to no one in particular and took a deep gulp. She pushed a bowl of crisps towards me. I took one, but crisp it wasn't. It tasted like salted paper.

She was staring out of the window as she wiped a cloth across the bar where she had spilt the drink. 'If it rains much more today we'll need a boat to get home.' She spoke Italian with a southern accent. It sounded Neapolitan to me, with the usual sawn-off consonants. No point finishing a word if you knew what was coming.

I looked over my shoulder at the damp street. You could only see umbrellas walking past. I nodded and took another gulp. 'I prefer my liquids on the inside.'

'Want another?' She was pouring it before I had even replied.

'Thanks.'

I sat there for a few minutes, watching the rain. I didn't want to rush it. Go in too quick and people know you're pumping them for information rather than making idle conversation.

'What happened to that prosciuttificio?' I asked eventually.

'Lombardi?'

'That's the one.'

'He sold up about a year ago.'

'I was looking for it just now, couldn't see it anywhere. Thought I had lost my head.'

'The only thing they're selling there now are flats.'

'I saw all that building work and thought I must have been on the wrong road.'

'Right place,' she said, 'just a year or so too late.'

I took another gulp of the malvasia. 'He still in business?'

'Who? Lombardi?'

'Yeah.'

She put her chin in the air. 'Boh. I wouldn't know.'

'You got a phone book?'

She turned around and reached under the table where the

till was. 'Ecco.' She put it in front of me, turning it round so it was the right way up. 'Another?'

I heard her pouring the wine as I leafed through the phone book. There were two or three pages of Lombardis. More than half a column of Carlo Lombardis. I turned to the front of the book where the commercial section was and looked for prosciuttifici. Quite a few of those too, but there he was: Carlo Lombardi. He had moved out of town, towards Colorno. I wrote down the address and passed the phone book back to her. I left a note on the bar and walked back to the car, my legs feeling a little frizzanti.

I drove to the address of the new prosciuttificio. It was easy enough to see: this time there were all the usual yellow posters with prices and weights. I went in and smelt the musty, peppery smell of seasoned meat. There were hundreds of tear-shaped legs hanging from the ceiling. Eventually a man in a white overcoat came towards me. He had thinning white hair swept back and glasses hanging around his neck. I noticed his chin was slightly skew, so that when he smiled a greeting his lips made a thin figure of eight. It had the effect of making him look cheerful or boyish.

'You Lombardi?' I asked.

'Certainly am,' he said.

'Didn't you use to have the place over on Via Pordenone?'

'Used to. Not any more.' He put his glasses on and looked at me as if he were trying to recognise an old customer. 'We've been here almost nine months now.'

I nodded, looking around quickly to check we were still on our own.

'What can I get you?' he asked.

I shook my head. 'I'm not here to buy. I wanted to ask you a few questions.'

He looked confused. 'Go on.'

'Your car got torched a while back.'

'That was a long time ago,' he said slowly. 'How do you know about that?'

I passed him my card. I watched him read it and then look up at me with a frown.

'A client of mine had his car torched the night before last. I was wondering if there's a connection.'

'A client?'

'Yeah, a client. Someone who doesn't take kindly to intimidation.'

We looked at each other with suspicion.

'Dozens of people get their cars burnt each year,' he said. 'Why come to me?'

'Because you sold up soon after. Made me wonder what went on. Made me wonder whether anyone suggested you move on. Whether you got any threatening phone calls, saying it was a good time to sell, that your family would be safer someplace else.'

His eyes narrowed and he was nodding slightly. 'Wait here,' he said. He walked through a side door behind the counter and a little while later came back with a woman. 'My wife will watch the shop,' he said. He had taken off his white coat. He beckoned me round the side of the counter and led me through the side door into a little office, crowded with files and papers.

We both sat down. The place was so small that we had to dovetail our knees.

'What's this about?' he said, staring at me.

'I told you. My client's car was torched a couple of days ago. I came across your name in the records . . .'

'Which records?'

'Fire department.'

We stared at each other some more. He took out a cigarette and started turning it from a solid into a gas.

'I'm trying to work out a pattern.'

'And who are you?'

The guy was clearly nervous. He had something he wanted to share, but wasn't sure he should be sharing it with me. I told him who I was, gave him the names of a couple of reputable Carabinieri who could vouch for me. He nodded, nothing more.

'I saw the building site where you used to be. Looks like they're going to make a killing.' I watched him drag on his cigarette. 'How many flats are they building there? Twenty-five, thirty probably. Six floors, one on each corner. A couple up top. Something like that. Each one eighty metres square. Say six or seven thousand euros a metre.' I whistled. My maths wasn't good enough to work it out, but it was millions. 'How much did you sell out for? Two, three hundred thousand?'

He blew smoke towards the ceiling, shaking his head. He stared at me as if trying to decide whether to talk or not. 'You know,' he started quietly, 'sometimes I hate this country. We were blessed with the most beautiful landscape in Europe. Mountains, sea, rivers. Everywhere you look it's stunning. But we're slowly ruining it.' He crushed his cigarette into a green glass ashtray. 'There's barely a beach left that's public, hardly anywhere you can sit down on a bit of sand without someone hassling you for five or ten euros. They're building huge marinas in every tiny fishing village. The mountainsides are dotted with illegal villas. The traffic jams just to get there make you want to turn round.'

'It's the same everywhere,' I said.

'No. No, it's not. There's something different in this country. Rules here are like breadsticks. As soon as you get them out of the packaging, you realise someone else has already broken them. You see that they're in pieces and if they're going to serve their purpose, they've got to be broken some more.'

'It's the same everywhere,' I said again.

'Bullshit. Here the rules don't mean anything. Everything in this country is a façade, a mask, a pretence. If you ever get behind the façade, if you ever get through all the flowery phrases about "re-evaluation of the territory", you'll see the usual thieves and gangsters after a quick buck.'

I gave a tired nod of my head, not wanting to contradict a man in pain. I let him keep talking for a while and listened to his bitterness.

'This city', he lowered his voice slightly, 'is like my wife's waistline. It spreads out every year. Every year it grows. It's relentless, there's nothing you can do to stop it. Just a year ago that spot out there', he thumbed over his shoulder through a tiny window, 'was agricultural land. Now look.'

I leant left and right and could see the familiar triangular arm of a gyrating crane. It looked like a transparent Toblerone.

'More flats and cars and kitchens and consumption and pollution and . . .'

'People have got to have somewhere to live,' I said.

'Ha!' He looked at the ceiling again. 'That old defence. The oldest in the book. "People have got to have somewhere to live." Of course they do. You would have thought I was denying them bread. Of course they've got to have somewhere to live. But they don't need two places to live. Or three or four. We've got a declining population but we're still building at breakneck speeds. Almost everyone in this country has two homes, some have three or four. It's not about having homes, it's about greed.'

I nodded as he drew breath.

'The politicians have all sorts of euphemisms. They call it recupero. Valorizzazione del territorio. Ripristino. Riqualificazione. They make it sound like they're transforming ugly wastelands into green parks where children will play happily on swings and slides until sunset. But it's just old-fashioned sviluppo, frenetic development. It's all about building, pouring cement onto greenfield sites, spreading the city outwards until there's no countryside left.'

When he had finished I asked him what any of it had to do with his car.

'Someone was trying to persuade me to sell,' he said. 'Someone wanted me out.'

'Did they say so explicitly?'

'Very.'

'Like?'

'What you said just now. Late-night calls, saying the area was dangerous, that now would be a good time to sell and so on.'

'Male?'

31

He nodded.

'Remember much about the voice?'

'Nothing. Just menace.' He stared at me. He took out another cigarette but simply held it between his fingers with the lighter in his other hand. He pointed the unlit cigarette at me. 'You know what a "piano regolatore" is?'

I shook my head, but it sounded familiar, like one of those many plans politicians come up with. Piano urbanistico, piano turismo, piano regolatore.

'It's the development document for the city,' he said. 'It tells you where the city is going to sprawl next. Tells you what area of agricultural land is going to be buried in cement, which greenfield sites are going to be gone for ever.'

'Doesn't sound like you approve.'

He shook his head fast. 'Someone knew my place was going to come inside the boundaries of the new development belt. That's why they were desperate to get hold of it. It was suddenly, as they say, appetibile. It was going to be more lucrative than an oil well. If you're inside the belt you can apply for a cambio di destinazione d'uso, which means you can convert anything to residential use. If I had known that, I would have held on to it. The value of the place would have tripled or more. Instead I sold out for next to nothing.'

'To Masi Costruzione?'

He shook his head and looked at me as if I had offended him. 'I'm not that stupid.'

'How do you mean?'

'If a constructor comes to you wanting to buy land you know something's up. You know he thinks he'll be able to build and you know you can ask for a fortune. I've never met

32

Masi. I just had a guy approach me who said he wanted to take over the business.'

'When was this?'

'A few weeks after the car went. This guy wanted to run a prosciuttificio. I didn't connect the car and the calls with him. He just seemed to come at the right time and he was offering good money for a quick sale. I only realised later why he was in such a rush.'

'Because the new piano regolatore was about to be made public?'

'Exactly. Like I said, if I had known my place was inside the development belt I would have held out for double or treble what he was offering.'

'What was he called?'

'Luciano something.' He was shaking his head again. 'The minute I sold it to him, the whole thing was passed on to Masi, the planning permits went through, and almost before I had moved my stuff out, the cranes were there, ready to rumble.'

'This Luciano,' I said, 'you remember his surname?'

He shook his head. 'It'll be in the Ufficio del Catasto.'

I nodded. 'One other thing. What was the insurance company?'

'For the car?'

I nodded.

'Gruppo Sicurezza.'

'And they provided a replacement?'

He threw his eyes to the ceiling. 'Eventually.'

We disentangled our knees and he led me back out to the shop. He told his wife to slice me a few etti of culatello. She started up the machine and moved the circular blade backwards and forwards, catching the thin wafers in something that looked like a crocodile clip. She wrapped it up in aluminium foil and gave it to me with a warm smile. I asked them what I owed, but they both tutted to say it was on the house.

Lombardi walked me to the door. 'If you find the people who did this,' he looked at me anxiously, 'what happens to my car?'

'How do you mean?'

'If the insurance company find out there's someone else who should have footed the bill, you can be sure they'll ask for their money back.'

I reassured him that I would make sure his car didn't get taken away. He started telling me why he needed it, how his grandchildren lived forty kilometres away and the only way to get there was in a car. His wife didn't have one, and if the insurance company was intending to stop him seeing his grandchildren, he would hold me responsible. I held up a hand and told him to trust me.

Amedeo Masi's office wasn't far away. It was the next exit on the ring road. Outside it there was a sign with the Masi logo, big white letters on an oval, blue background. The office was on the ground floor of a block of flats. I assumed he had built the whole block and kept the ground floor for himself.

I got buzzed in and saw that there was nothing more than a couple of rooms with a couple of desks. It all looked fairly drab for the control centre of a construction empire. I guessed Masi was the kind of man who liked to keep costs down.

The young girl on the front desk was sturdy with short black hair and a chunky kind of face. She frowned at me when I said I didn't have an appointment. I gave her my card and she disappeared into another office. As she opened the door I could hear the booming tones of a man who was losing his temper. She came out again, shutting the door. 'You'll have to wait a while, I'm afraid.'

'Was that Masi I heard shouting?'

'That was him.' She nodded.

'Does he often raise his voice?'

'Never lowers it,' she said, smiling naturally, like she almost admired him for it.

'Must be hard to work with.'

'And live with.'

I looked at her sideways.

'I'm his daughter,' she explained. 'I don't even notice it any more.'

I nodded at her and went to sit down. I listened to the phones. They were ringing constantly. No sooner had someone hung up than one rang again. It was so frenetic it was almost tiring to listen to. The receptionist and another girl were ordering materials, phoning banks, talking to contractors and employees.

Eventually, a short man came out of the closed office. He was stocky with a flat nose and a round stomach. As he got closer I could see his face looked like a crushed beer can: a strange combination of the sharp and the smooth. His hair was slightly ginger and the freckles on his face had joined forces a decade ago, leaving him with an orangey-brown complexion.

'Masi,' he said gruffly, holding out his hand as I stood up. 'What's this about?'

'Can we talk in private?'

'Like that, is it?' he said, snarling at me as he turned to walk back towards his office. He held the door open for me as I went in, then shut it and stood there with his hands on his hips.

'Allora?' His body language suggested that he was impatient to get on with his day.

'I'm investigating a fire in a car park a few nights ago.'

He nodded, the sides of his mouth pulled down in disapproval. 'What's that got to do with me?'

I explained the connection: the fact that another car had been torched some time ago. That Lombardi had sold up after a bad fire and a good offer. How he had started to receive unpleasant phone calls. Masi frowned when he heard about Lombardi, pushing his head back like he was trying to place the name. 'Doesn't mean anything to me,' he said quickly, like he had really tried his best.

'Lombardi used to own a prosciuttificio on Via Pordenone. He sold the land to someone called Luciano, who sold the land to you. Now you're building a block of flats there.'

'Via Pordenone?'

'That's right.'

We stared at each other.

'So you've come in here to ask if I'm in the habit of setting fire to the property of people from whom I intend to buy land?'

I shrugged as if to ask him to answer his own question.

'Sit down,' he said, motioning to a chair with a headbutt to the air. He sat down behind his desk and studied me. 'You've come in here with some pretty serious accusations.'

'I'm not making any accusations. Just asking you to tell me what you know.'

'It wouldn't take long to tell you everything I know. I'm a simple man.'

'Tell me everything then.'

He stared at me some more. 'You know much about building?'

I shook my head.

'It's a very simple process. You buy land, you build houses or offices or airports or whatever, and you sell them.

37

Straightforward. All you need is land, labour, materials. A bit of expertise and experience, and up it goes.'

'And capital,' I said.

'Yes. And capital. Lots of it. Are you going to accuse me of being a capitalist as well?'

'No accusation,' I said, throwing my left palm in the air, fingers up. 'I just know that you need a lot of capital to put up a block of flats.'

'Sure you do,' he said, 'but I started with nothing. The only money I've ever had behind me is what I put in my back pocket myself, you with me? I started out as an apprentice when I was fifteen. I've worked every day since then. Every day. For years, if a worker didn't show, I used to do their shift. I would still do it today if I had time. Look at me.' He showed me his calloused hands. 'Do I look like a lazy capitalist?'

'No, no you don't,' I said slowly.

He stared at me and nodded. 'I've been lucky, I've made a lot of money.' He moved his hands so that his palms faced the ceiling, a gesture to suggest there was nothing dishonest in his wealth. 'But I've given work to hundreds of people, given flats to—'

'Sold, I assume.'

He shot me a glance as a reproach for the interruption. 'I've sold flats to thousands of people. Flats that are safe, comfortable, good value for money. Look at the resale value of a Masi flat. It's a great investment because everything works, everything has been thought through and done properly. My name is an assurance of quality. I've never left an invoice unpaid. I've never failed to pay a worker. I've never

38

salted away millions and feigned bankruptcy. You ask any supplier if they've ever had difficulty with me. You won't hear a bad word.'

He was talking faster, still trying to defend himself from my sideways accusation.

'I've worked hard,' he went on. 'And I've helped other people work hard. People seem to think that working in construction is a licence to print money. You know what? It's hard, hard work. It's expensive, gruelling work.' He showed me his rough hands again, then ran them over his desk, his palms brushing the papers that were strewn everywhere. 'I'm not much different to any other labourer. I make more money, sure, but I work as hard as any of them. Harder.'

I nodded. I wanted to give him his head, let him vent a bit of pride.

'The problem with this country', he went on, 'is that everyone resents success. If you sweat to build and nurture a company, if it grows and becomes successful, people point at you and start insinuating you're bent, like you must have made compromises on the way. That's the malice of envy. It allows people to think that the only reason they're shabby is because they're honest. Listen, I don't deny I'm financially comfortable. I'm well off.' He waved an arm around the room. On the walls there were photographs of himself in a hard hat shaking hands with dignitaries wearing tricolour sashes hanging obliquely across their chests. 'Where's the harm in being well off? I'm proud I've been successful, and even more proud to have helped hundreds of other people enjoy success.'

He was looking at me now, trying to work out if his words

had sunk in. 'So what's this all about? You said there's been some fire.'

'Right. No accident either. It was arson.'

He was nodding slowly. 'And you say the same thing happened over in Via Pordenone?'

'The pattern was the same. Car set alight. Late-night intimidation.'

He looked at the ceiling the way some people ask for heavenly intervention. It looked false somehow, like the outrage or piety was manufactured. He snapped back to his usual self, fixing me with a stare and leaning forward on his desk. 'Via Pordenone was a bad bit of business for us. I don't often make mistakes, but that was a big one. I overpaid for it. Bought it at the top of the market a year ago and even if we manage to sell all the flats tomorrow we'll be lucky to cover our costs on it.'

'Who did you buy it from?'

He looked at his desk and shook his head. 'I really can't remember.'

'I'm sure a successful businessman like you finds it hard to forget the bad deals. I heard you bought from a Luciano somebody. Ring any bells?'

'I do a dozen deals a month, hundreds in a year. I don't remember every person I shake hands with.'

Most businessmen I've met remember every detail of every deal: the figures, the people, the circumstances, the coincidences. Each deal has an anecdote or two. I didn't buy his memory lapse.

'And did you know this Luciano character? Had you ever met him before?'

'I don't even know who you're talking about.' He said it like his confusion, or my insistence, made him angry.

'Luciano, the person you bought Via Pordenone from. Did you know him?'

'I told you . . .' he started.

'And when you bought the land, did it already have planning permission?'

He looked at me with contempt. 'I don't buy land without it. What do you think I am, some kind of farmer?'

'Would you have any objection to me asking your office', I thumbed over my shoulder, 'to look out the paperwork, find me a name?'

'They're busy,' he whispered, staring at me in defiance. 'So am I.' Any friendliness he had was gone and his whisper seemed more intimidating than his shouts.

'You don't understand why this is important?'

He had stood up and his hands were by his sides as if he were about to shoo me out of his office. 'I don't like mud-slingers,' he said, headbutting the air with the side of his head again to show me which direction to walk.

'I'm not slinging mud,' I said, staring back at him. 'Just trying to understand who is burning cars.'

'I can't help you there. I build flats. That's all I do. I'm just a simple builder.' He moved to the door.

As I walked past him I could feel his animal energy, like he was ready to attack. I stood in front of him for a split second, to let him know that I had that sort of energy myself. I headed out and heard the door slam behind me.

The Ufficio del Catasto was the local land registry office, the kind of place where time seemed to slow down. Like a lot of the people in public offices, they appeared to have been expelled from charm school a long time ago. You stood waiting by a window for ages before anyone even came by, and when they did they walked past without looking at you. You could spend a lifetime in there before you met something called service. If you succeeded in getting their attention, they gave the impression of being disturbed and irritated, like you had woken them up from an enjoyable dream.

The only way to get the information I needed was to waft a couple of fifties in the air. A surly man who had taken pleasure in ignoring me for a long time found his smile all of a sudden. 'Via Pordenone, you say?'

'Number 17. I'm interested in the owner who came between Lombardi Carlo and Masi Amedeo.'

He scribbled down the names and disappeared through a small door. I went and sat down on a plastic chair. They had a couple of old copies of *Bell'Italia* on a table and I picked one up. It had stunning photographs of emerald coves and mountain peaks and strong stallions in gentle meadows. It made me think about everything Lombardi had said, about how our peninsula was so blessed with beauty. Beauty in this country is like the ice on a lake in spring, so fragile and thin that as soon as you touch it the whole surface will splinter and crack, and you'll fall into the cold, dark waters beneath. We're obsessed by beauty because it allows us to escape the terrors of life, it allows us to cover up the brutal realities. We're illusionists, battling against ageing and death. It's a way of life, an attempt to defy decay. We beautify ourselves and our houses incessantly to make them appear nobler, stronger, more civilised, to make life appear fairer and kinder. But then you begin to realise that behind the pristine flat lies a burnt-out shell of a car, that our obsession with looking good is actually an attempt to look away, to ignore reality. We don't want to see things as they really are. We would rather have good-looking lies than the dull, ugly truth. That's how we ended up with the politicians we've got. We prefer fantasy to fact.

'Scusi.' The man was back with a piece of paper and was knocking on the glass. 'Ecco.'

He passed a slip of paper underneath the window. I read the name: Luciano Tosti. There was an address too. I pushed the two bank notes towards him and flashed him a false smile.

As I walked down the wide staircase I looked at the name. It meant nothing to me. The address was somewhere in Milan.

It took me a couple of hours to get there. The place was in a nondescript suburb. Every balcony had Inter or Milan flags hanging on its railings. Black and blue and red and black. I parked up and found the right block. I stood outside the building looking at the buzzers and there was no Tosti. I assumed the man at the Ufficio del Catasto must have given me the wrong address. I buzzed another name at random. No one answered. I held down another, but still nothing. I stepped back and waited. Either way the pavement was deserted. No one appeared to be coming in or out of the building. I rang all the buzzers one after the other. Eventually someone squawked 'Chi è'?

I told her I was looking for Luciano Tosti. She didn't say anything. I repeated what I had said and heard her calling a man's name.

'Who is this?' A gruff voice came on.

I told him my name and that I was trying to find Luciano Tosti. 'I haven't seen him for years,' I said, which wasn't, after all, a lie. 'I used to be at school with him,' I went on, which was.

'I better come down,' the man said.

A few minutes later I heard the front gate click. I looked up and saw an elderly man walking towards me, head down. He struggled to pull the gate open on his own, so I stepped forward and tried to help him. It was so well sprung that it almost knocked him sideways as it started to shut.

'What did you say your name was?' he asked.

I told him and he looked at me with suspicion. 'I thought you said you were at school with Luciano.'

I didn't know what to say, so I nodded as if confirming it.

'You look older than him,' he said.

I ran a hand across my short, greying hair. 'To be honest, it was my younger brother who was at school with him.'

He was still looking at me sideways. 'And what is it you're after?'

'My brother's ill. Very ill. And he's asked me to contact a few of his old friends before . . . you know, before . . .'

44

At the mention of illness the man seemed to soften. He looked at me and nodded. 'I don't talk in front of citofoni,' he said, glancing at the box of buzzers. He started walking slowly along the pavement. 'It was an ugly thing,' he said, stopping to look at me. 'A very ugly thing.'

'What was?'

'What happened to Tosti.' He looked at me again, as if to make sure that I really was as ignorant as I sounded.

'What happened?'

He stared at me as if preparing me for bad news. 'He was killed. Killed right here.' The old man pointed at the ground. We were just in front of a larger gate which sloped downwards to the block of flats's garages.

'When was this?'

'Less than a year ago. He was sitting in his car, just waiting for these gates to open and they . . .' He tailed off.

I looked around. It was strange how normal the place felt, like a battlefield decades later that becomes just a field again. There was no hint of the blood-spilling, no sign of anything out of the ordinary. The yellow light above the gate started flashing and the man stepped back as the gate began to open in automated jerks. I moved to the other side and we watched a car drive in.

We came back together as the gate started to shut. 'Did they ever find the person responsible?'

He smiled briefly. 'You know what it's like. They accused plenty of people but convicted no one.'

'Who was accused?'

'Mah!' he said like he didn't believe any of it. 'They said he was involved in big money deals.' He shook his head.

45

'You don't believe it?'

His shoulders rose slowly like they were being inflated. 'He always seemed, excuse me saying this of the dead, he always seemed a little sfigato, you know? From what I heard, he struggled to pay the ground rent each year. He always paid late if he paid at all. He drove around in an old Fiat Duna.' The man laughed gently at the memory and shook his head. 'He just, he didn't seem like the sort of person who would be making big deals.'

'Who said he was?'

He looked at me through narrowed eyes. 'You're asking a lot of questions. I thought you were only looking for an old schoolfriend.'

He had the honest intensity of a good man smelling a rat and I didn't like being the rat. I told him why I was really there, told him that I was investigating property deals a while back in a nearby city. He stared at me in surprise, like he didn't know whether to be offended or excited by the revelation.

'Why', I said slowly, not wanting to rush the questions, 'did you say he was involved in financial deals?'

'Something his widow said. Said he had come into a lot of money.'

I looked up at the block of flats behind him. There was a woman on a balcony hanging out her laundry. 'Does his widow still live here?'

He shook his head. 'They moved away.'

'They?'

'She had a little boy. She was called Rosaria something. Can't recall the surname, but she's from down south. Nice girl.'

'Where did they move to?'

'No idea. Can't blame them though. It must have been terrible, seeing this spot every day.' He grimaced and pointed at the pavement again as if there were still blood down there.

'Did she leave a forwarding address?'

'You would have to ask the administrator.'

'Who's that?'

'Giancarlo.'

'He in?'

He led me back towards the citofono. He buzzed Giancarlo and we went into his apartment. He fussed around looking through his files and eventually came up with a piece of paper. 'Ecco,' he said, pulling on his glasses. 'It's not exactly a forwarding address. Just a note to say any post can be left for her at some shop. Carla's Intimo, Via della Salute.'

The shop was a few blocks away. I had to stop a woman to ask her where exactly and she pointed me in the right direction. Carla's was the cheap end of the underwear market. The window displayed rows of knickers and bras and pyjamas that seemed to have lost their colours in the sun. Inside, the place felt unexpectedly like a library. There were boxes piled high on neat shelves behind the counter and in front of them there was an old wooden stepladder.

'Buongiorno,' said a dark-haired woman as I walked in. She was half-way up the ladder so that her waist was at eye level.

'I'm looking for Rosaria,' I said.

'Join the club,' she said without humour. She stared at me. Her dark eyes had a very slight squint.

'A lot of people looking for her?'

'Were a while back.'

'You know why?'

'Who are you?'

'Name's Castagnetti. I'm a private detective. I'm trying to work out what happened to her husband.'

'Or to his money?'

'What money?'

She snorted like she didn't believe my ignorance. 'Why do you care what happened to her husband?'

'Did I say I cared?'

She looked at me with disdain.

'I'm trying to find out what happened to him because his name came up in an investigation I'm involved in. I traced him to a block around the corner and then found out he was killed a while back. That kind of thing arouses my curiosity.'

She started folding a pair of knickers into a box like her mind was elsewhere.

'Where will I find Rosaria?' I insisted.

She put the lid on the box and turned around to insert it in one of the stacks behind her. Then she turned back towards me and shook her head. 'Rosaria doesn't want to be found.'

'Doesn't she want justice?'

She laughed at the silly idealism of the question and started walking up the first step of the ladder. 'She wants to be left alone.'

'Give her this.' I gave her one of my cards. 'If she cares about justice for her husband, tell her to get in touch.'

The woman looked at it, looked at me and nodded. She put the card between two fingers and flicked it onto the counter. It fell off and I reached down to pick it up and put it back on the counter.

I stood there watching her. She was dark and feisty and looked like a strong woman. Her accent was from the south somewhere. She kept walking up and down the ladder, putting underwear in boxes and inserting them into the stacks, resolutely ignoring me.

'Allora?' she said impatiently, as if she was demanding to know what I was still doing there.

I was about to go to the door when I heard a voice from the inside of the shop. 'Rosaria, come here a minute.'

The woman up the ladder froze, looking at me. The voice called her again and since it didn't get a reply, the body behind it walked into the shop: a small, tense-looking woman who I imagined was the boss.

'Buongiorno,' she said, looking me over. 'I'm sorry, I didn't realise we had a customer. Can I help?'

'You just have.'

'Excuse me?'

'I was just looking for Rosaria.'

The small woman looked over at her assistant. Rosaria descended the ladder slowly, her head held back like she was still feeling defiant.

'What do you want?' she said, staring at me with her black eyes.

Her boss looked from Rosaria to me, feeling the tension.

'Just what I said. I want to ask you a couple of questions.'

'Why?'

I explained to her how I had come across her husband. Told her about the fire at Bragantini's factory and the possible link to Via Pordenone. Her chin was in the air whilst I was talking, her bottom lip jutting out like she was still suspicious of me. When I had said my piece she stood there, staring at me with her hands on her hips. After a couple of seconds she dropped her hands to her sides as if she had given up on resisting. She turned to her boss like she was asking advice or permission.

'Why don't you go and have a quick coffee?' the older woman said, looking from Rosaria to me.

Rosaria went into the back to get her coat. Her boss and I were left alone and she smiled at me. 'She's been through a lot,' she whispered. 'She's a lovely girl, but she's lost all trust in people.'

I nodded, smiling at her silently as gratitude for the insight.

'He's still asleep,' Rosaria said, coming through the back door of the shop. 'Call me if he wakes up.'

'OK my dear.'

She walked past me and out of the door without saying anything. I caught up with her on the pavement and followed her. She turned into a bar on the corner and only when she was leaning on the curved chrome of the bar did she look at me.

'What are you having?'

'Coffee.'

'Two coffees,' she shouted at the barman.

'Subito,' he shouted back. 'Two coffees.'

We took them over to a table in the corner. There was a fruit machine next to the table that was making irritating noises. I could see the flashing lights reflecting on her shoulders.

'Allora?' she said again. 'What do you want exactly?'

'I want to find out who killed your husband.'

She didn't say anything, so I asked her the same question she had asked me. 'What do you want?'

'To be left alone.'

'You get bothered a lot?'

She didn't answer.

'Who's bothering you?'

'The same people who were hassling Luciano before he died.'

'Who's that?'

She snorted, looking at me with contempt. 'You're trying to broker a deal for them, right?'

'For who?' I couldn't follow what she was saying.

She stared at me and threw her coffee back. As she put the white tazzina back in the saucer she looked at me again and, for the first time, smiled. There was still a trace of contempt in her face, but she was genuinely amused as well. 'You really don't know anything?'

'I only found out that your husband got hurt five minutes ago.'

'Hurt?' she said scornfully. 'That's one way to put it.'

She was hard all right, but it was the kind of hardness that came from fragility. She seemed vulnerable despite that tough exterior, like an animal defending its young in the wild. The sort that would suddenly turn on you when you weren't even threatening her.

We sat there in silence for a while. I watched the jingling fruit machine spill colours at her back: lime green, bright orange. It kept making its demented tune. At least, I thought, it would keep our conversation private. If we ever got some conversation.

'How old's your boy?' I said softly.

She looked at me like she was about to lash out to protect him, but she closed her eyes wearily. 'Almost two.'

'And you have him with you there in the shop?'

She nodded. 'La signora is very good to me. She looks after him half the time. She gave us a room above the shop. She was widowed too about a year ago, more or less the same time that Luciano was killed. We sort of found each other. I had gone there before a few times, so we knew each other vaguely, but one day, soon after it happened, I went in to buy something and I stayed there all day, just talking things through with her. By the end of the day, she had invited us to stay in her spare room and had offered me a part-time job.'

'Kind woman.'

She nodded slowly, staring beyond me to the outside world.

I moved the tazzina round in its saucer, waiting for the right time to ask her about her husband.

'You know,' she started without prompting, 'for a while they thought I had done it.' She put her head sideways.

'That's always their first thought. Bound to be the spouse.'

'Built up quite a case against me.' She exhaled in derision, her smile turning into a bitter grimace. 'Luciano had come into some money. The first time in his life. He was flush. They thought,' her voice wobbled for an instant, 'they thought I had killed him, or had him killed, for the money.' Her lower lip was quivering now.

'What money?' I asked quietly.

Her sigh sounded more like a growl. She pulled her hands apart, then put them back together. She shrugged, then looked at me shaking her head. 'It was some stupid investment scam. The only investment in his life that ever went well. Trouble was, it wasn't his money and it wasn't his scam. He was just the frontman.'

'I don't follow.'

'He was lent money to buy a business.'

'A prosciuttificio?'

'How did you know?' She looked at me suddenly, surprised and scared.

'That's how I got his name. From the Ufficio del Catasto.'

'So you know all about it?'

'Hardly anything. I know he bought the joint and sold it to Masi Costruzioni.'

'That's just about all I know,' she said with regret. 'That and the fact that he bought the place with someone else's money.'

'How did you find that out?'

She laughed bitterly. 'Wasn't hard. Luciano never had money of his own to speak of. I knew he couldn't afford to buy a beer, let alone a whole business. Someone put him up to it.'

'He was someone's stooge?'

She nodded. 'Only,' she hesitated, 'he started getting ideas that he wasn't. The place he bought was placed inside the residential land belt a few months later, and he realised he was the legal owner of a goldmine. He thought he could make a lot of money and he did. He sold it to Masi Costruzioni for a huge profit.'

'Only it wasn't his money in the first place?'

She shook her head, closing her eyes as if to try and blank out the memory. 'Luciano thought he had hit the big-time. He said it was time to pack our bags. Said we had enough money to live on for a few years. He wanted to go to Spain.' She put her forehead into the palm of her hand and stayed in that position for a few seconds, her shoulders bouncing like she was coughing silently.

It sounded like her man had tried to trouser money that belonged to someone else and had paid the ultimate price. I asked her who had lent him the money and she rolled her eyes.

'That's what the authorities wanted to know. After his death, that's what they asked me. I told them I had no idea, but they found out.'

'And?'

'It was some bank. You should ask the Carabinieri.'

'I will. Who was in charge of the case?'

'Speranza. Never seemed very in charge to me,' she said with bitterness.

It sounded like a good lead. I looked at her and wondered if she was strong or honest enough to talk about her husband as something other than just a victim. I assumed that if he had bought the place he had had some hand in lighting the fires and making the threatening calls. I tried to ask the question as tactfully as possible.

'The man who sold his prosciuttificio to your husband was subjected to arson attacks and threatening phone calls.'

'So I heard,' she said curtly.

'Did Luciano ever talk about that?'

She shook her head. 'That's not possible.'

'What's not possible?'

'That Luciano would ever threaten anyone. If anything it was the opposite.'

'What do you mean?'

'Luciano was getting some heat himself.'

'Meaning?'

'When he sold the place on, a man came round here,

shouting at him, threatening him, calling late at night. That sort of thing.'

'Who was it?'

She shrugged.

'Did you ever see him?'

She nodded.

'And you would recognise him again?'

'Of course,' she said quickly as if the question were stupid.

'What did he look like?'

'An accountant. He didn't look like the normal kind of thug.'

'And what did Luciano do?'

'He laughed it off. Said it was nothing, just some sfigato who was jealous of our success.' So far she had confirmed what I already suspected. Masi was being tipped off about lucrative land deals. But he couldn't make the purchase himself. His name was too well known. If he had stepped forward to make a deal, everyone would have known land was about to be redesignated and he would have had to pay through the teeth. So he was using frontmen. They bought the land and then sold it on to him. Masi had to trust those frontmen to sell at the price he wanted. But when Tosti found himself the proud owner of valuable land, he had started to think he had finally made it. He was dreaming of zeros in his bank account and had tried, like many before him, to take them to some sandy beach abroad. That's why, presumably, he had taken a hit.

'How much money did your husband make on the deal?'

She looked up at me as if she didn't understand.

'It must have come to you when he died.'

56

She shrugged.

'So?'

'He left me almost a hundred thousand.'

'You're a lucky woman,' I said with more sarcasm than I intended. It was the wrong thing to say and she stared at me with scorn.

'I'm a widow. I have no home and my son has no father. I don't want that money. I don't know where it comes from or where it belongs.'

'So why not give it back?'

'To who? To the first person who threatens my family? To someone who might be responsible for my husband's death? Who should I give it to?'

I didn't say anything. She stared at me with her large black eyes as if it were my fault. I couldn't give her a reply. She pushed back her thick hair and growled a sigh.

'What do you think I would rather have? My husband or the filthy money that cost him his life?'

I nodded, not needing to reply to the rhetorical question. 'Before all this happened,' I said slowly, 'had you ever heard of Amedeo Masi? Did Luciano ever talk about him?'

She shook her head brusquely like it was all useless. She was looking at the floor and I took the chance to study her face again. It seemed on the cusp between beauty and sadness. Her large, dark eyes were framed by a permanent, almost imperceptible, frown.

'Where did you meet him?' I asked quietly.

She didn't move, but started smiling slightly. 'Monteleccio.'

'Where's that?'

'Somewhere in the Apennines. A tiny town way up in the

mountains.' She looked at me and then stared at her hands. 'We had gone there for some sagra. I can't remember what it was. Some cheap wine and food festival, and a couple of friends and I had nothing better to do. He was in the queue behind us with a few of his friends. You know what it's like. They were talking and joking, we were pretending to ignore them. In the end we sat at the same table and things just went from there.' She closed her eyes, like she was trying to see the whole scene again. 'I should get back,' she said abruptly, as if she were embarrassed at having wasted time in useless reminiscing.

I walked her back to the shop and told her I would do what I could. She shrugged like she expected nothing but trouble.

The Carabinieri caserma was a smart palazzo a few blocks away. In the courtyard there were half a dozen black cars with the oblique red stripe. There was an armed guard outside, a sign that the state here is still on a war footing against organised crime and home-grown terrorism.

I was pointed towards the front desk and asked to see Speranza. He was out, and I was told to sit in a waiting room. There were two other people in there who looked bored.

An hour later a harsh voice called my name. I stood up and followed the man down a corridor, up some steps, along another corridor. The man accompanying me kept saying hello to people he passed.

'Ecco,' he said, knocking very loudly on a wooden door.

'Avanti,' I heard from inside.

The man opened the door and I was shown in to a large office. I could tell Speranza was high-ranking just by the size of the room. There was an old, threadbare carpet thrown over the marble floor. Rising to greet me was a man with thick blond hair who held out his hand.

'Speranza, piacere,' he said.

'Castagnetti,' I said as I moved towards the chair he had pointed towards.

'You wanted to see me?'

I nodded. 'I'm a private investigator,' I said tentatively.

Most Carabinieri don't take kindly to my profession. They find we get in their way and, occasionally, steal their glory.

He nodded silently.

'I'm here about an old case.'

'Plenty of those. Which one?'

'Luciano Tosti.' I looked at him briefly. 'He was killed last year.'

He raised his eyebrows. 'I remember.' He cocked his head. 'What's your interest?'

'I was investigating a couple of cases of arson back home and one of them led me to Tosti. So I came round here today hoping to ask him a couple of questions but I find he was whacked last year. It kind of made me curious.'

He looked at me through his eyebrows. 'You want to tell me about these fires?'

'If you'll tell me about Tosti.'

He snorted a laugh.

I told him about the case, what little I knew: that Tosti had been the frontman for a construction company called Masi that wanted to buy land which was about to be redesignated. That he had got a taste for being a landowner and rebelled against his puppeteers. Speranza listened distractedly, turning round to type something into his computer as if I weren't there.

'We heard about that,' he said when I had finished. 'We figured it just like you said. We pursued it for a while but the curtain came down pretty quickly.'

'What do you mean?'

He pushed his head back and rolled it left and right like he was trying to remove a crick in his neck. 'Pressure from above.'

'The investigation was shut down?'

He tutted like I was an errant schoolchild. 'It's never put that way. We're simply told there are other priorities.' He mimicked an officious voice. 'Other leads to pursue. Other cases that need our time and resources.' The resentment was clear.

'How far did you go down the Masi line?'

'Far enough for it to get interesting. Tosti didn't turn out to be quite as much of a stooge as Masi had expected. Once Tosti was in possession of that prosciuttificio, and once he realised it was going to benefit from a cambio di destinazione d'uso, he realised he had something quite valuable. He started touting it around and Masi took exception. Masi had set up the deal in the first place, and to have Tosti betraying him like that must have got him pretty steamed up.'

'But Tosti sold it to him in the end?'

'Sure, but for a six-figure profit. He made Masi pay through the nose for something Masi thought was his in the first place. It must have been like finding your servant outside your house selling your silver.'

'And having to buy it back from him?'

The man nodded. 'We interviewed Masi once. He didn't seem like the sort of man to take it lying down.'

'He's quite a bulldozer, eh?'

'You've spoken to him too? Bulldozer's the word. The man looks like he's fought his way to the top.'

'And you think he fought Tosti?'

He bounced his head to the side. 'Wouldn't surprise me. He certainly sent some of his lackies to squeeze him. The widow told us about a man who was threatening him in the weeks before he was killed.'

61

'Who was that?'

'We never found out. Never traced him. Seems safe to assume he was a Masi missive.'

'Sounds like you had quite a case against him.'

'We did.' He stared blankly at his desk. 'We did. Trouble is, it was a case built on suspicions rather than facts.'

'No evidence?'

'Nothing. We knew he had been threatened a bit, but intimidation is a long way from murder. We never even found the murder weapon.'

'Which was?'

'Probably a hammer. He suffered some kind of blow to the temple. It was a very clean, circular blow. Surprisingly deep.'

'And no eyewitnesses, I assume?'

'None.'

We stared at each other like we were both in a cul-de-sac.

'Who lent him the money? Wasn't it some bank?'

'Yeah,' he said rolling his eyes like it was a source of suspicion, 'some bank. Tosti didn't have any collateral. Didn't have any earnings to speak of, and this bank lent him six figures to buy a big warehouse.'

'Which bank?'

'Investimenti Emiliani.'

'Never heard of it.'

'Me neither. We looked into it, but it was all straight. Nothing suspicious.'

'Apart from the fact they lent a loser the money in the first place.'

'Right.'

We looked at each other briefly.

'Who was behind it?'

'Investimenti Emiliani?'

'Right.'

'A guy called,' he put his chin on chest whilst trying to recall the name, 'Cesare Carini.'

'And who's he?'

'A banker. Investimenti Emiliani was his little sideline.'

'Where does he live?'

'Milan somewhere. Hang on.' He rooted through a large box file on his desk and pulled out a beige file. 'Via dei Mille, 107.'

'And you spoke to him?'

'Gave him a going over, sure. His explanation was that Tosti was some kind of informal società fiduciaria.'

'What does that mean?'

'That Carini wasn't really lending Tosti money at all. In layman's terms, Tosti was just administering the money on behalf of an unnamed third party.'

I frowned and Speranza leant closer, as if that would make the explanation more straightforward. 'People always use a fiduciaria to hide who the real beneficiary of a business is. It's the way they guarantee anonymity.'

'And you were satisfied with that explanation?'

'It made sense from Carini's point of view. He wasn't lending hundreds of thousands to a man whose only collateral was a Fiat Duna. He was lending it to the anonymous third party that Tosti was representing.'

'And I don't suppose Carini told you who stood behind Tosti?'

He shook his head.

'Nothing to do with Masi?'

'Not that we could work out.' He looked at his watch and leant forward, putting his palms down on his desk like he was about to stand and see me out.

'Just one last thing,' I said, staying where I was. 'The widow. Rosaria. Did she come under suspicion?'

'Sure. She came into Tosti's money when he died so she had a motive.'

'Did she have an alibi as well?'

'The night he was whacked she was in her flat.'

'On her own?'

'With her baby.'

'Not much of a witness.'

He shook his head. I stood up and we shook hands. He told me to get in touch if I needed anything.

I found Via Dei Mille and, at 107, a polished brass rectangle announcing the business called Investimenti Emiliani. I pressed the buzzer and a bored voice came on the line.

'Sì.'

'Cesare Carini?'

'Sì.'

'Mind if I come up?'

'Who are you?'

'I'm a private investigator.'

'Investigating what?' His voice sounded cautious.

'Arson.'

'I think you've got the wrong person. I can't help you.'

'The name Luciano Tosti mean anything to you?'

The line went quiet.

'You lent him the money to buy some land a year ago.'

His voice assumed a formal, defensive tone. 'I've spoken at length with the authorities about the case. I have nothing further to add.'

'The case is being reopened.'

'I'm glad,' he said hastily. 'I hope they find the person responsible.'

'You want to help me with that?'

'I lent him money.' The voice was losing its cool. 'That's all.'

The line went dead. I buzzed again but nothing happened. I took out one of my cards and posted it through the letter box.

I phoned a friend who worked in construction. He was one of those all-purpose labourers who's always doing a dozen jobs at the same time. Until recently he was earning more than a stockbroker.

'Spago? It's Casta.'

'Ciao grande. Come va?'

'Fine. You?'

'Still above ground. What can I do for you?'

'Let me take you out to lunch.'

'What's the catch?'

'I need to pick your brains.'

'You got tweezers?'

'Very funny. Bruno's at one?'

'Sure.'

I put my phone back in my pocket and started the drive back to Parma. I spent most of it thinking about Spago. He's an unusual character, one of those people who knows everyone and vice versa. Most people could recognise him just by his silhouette: an afro of grey curly hair that starts nearer the back of his head than the front. He always wears white overalls and drives around the city in a heavily dented pick-up full of bags of cement, bits of hose, random screws and keys and crowbars. He's an old-fashioned idealist, one of the last hard-core communists of Emilia-Romagna. He's always slagging off the careerist left-wingers as 'cashmere communists'. The worst they ever said about him is that he's naive.

'I've heard it's slow,' I said to him an hour later when he came into the bar, shouting hellos left and right. He had picked up a couple of flutes of malvasia from the barman on the way.

'Slow's not the word. It's static. I've got a couple of jobs to finish off and then nothing. No one's got any cash, or if they have they're keeping hold of it. The developers haven't sold even half the flats from last year and don't have the cashflow to invest in building new ones. So they're laying off hundreds of workers who are spending less money, cutting back on expensive restaurants and chic clothes. When the cranes aren't swinging the whole city suffers. People are struggling to buy a packet of cigarettes, let alone a new bilocale on the top floor of a swanky new block. Times are tight, and when times are tight the competition gets nasty.'

'You going to retire?'

'I've got two teenage daughters. They spend a hundred euros a week just on tights.'

'And only wear them once?'

'How did you know?' He laughed.

I looked at him laughing and smiled. Spago had always grumbled in the good times and was now laughing in the lean ones.

'You've heard the latest solution to the crisis?' He started chuckling again and shaking his head. 'They want to build an underground railway.'

'Where?'

'Here. In this little city. You could throw a stone from one

68

end to the other, but they want to build a metro.' He said it with scorn.

'Sounds like a decent idea,' I said, trying to wind him up. I shut the menu and passed it over to him.

'You are joking? Have you any idea how much money and time it will take to complete? Billions and billions of euros. Years and years of stop-start bullshit. The budget will go up every year as every politician dips their bread. And you know this used to be a Roman city? Every time they start drilling they'll find bones and pots and swords and mosaics, and everything will grind to a halt whilst archaeologists from all over the world pile in to examine the finds. It won't be finished until you and I are underground ourselves. And why do they want to build it anyway? To get from the railway station to the campus that little bit quicker? It's crazy.'

'Sounds sensible to me,' I said again.

He looked at me, about to rant once more, but saw me smiling and shook his head. 'Billions of euros. Billions and billions of euros of our taxes just so a few students can save three minutes of travelling time. Cazzo, why don't they just get out of bed a couple of minutes earlier?' He looked at me and shook his head again.

I smiled back and held up my glass. He picked up his and we clinked.

'To the underground,' I said.

'Cazzo,' he was still shaking his head, 'this city needs an underground like a fish needs fresh air.'

A waitress came to our table.

'For me the tortelli,' Spago said.

She looked at me.

69

'Risotto al limone please.'

'To drink?'

'Water. And something red. A gutturnio. As long as it's still. Or sangiovese.'

She nodded and went away and Spago continued his rant.

'They keep trying to improve this city and every time they try they lose something of the soul of the place. Look at la ghiaia. For centuries it's been a sort of trading pit. You know, you descended from the grandeur of the boulevards with their marble urns and pillars and pediments, and you walked down the steps into a democratic marketplace, our bustling souk where farmers and artisans could trade gossip and goods with the bourgeoisie and aristocrats. It was the one place in this city where everyone mixed, where the poorest immigrant rubbed shoulders with the fur-coated casalinga. It was where the poor went to buy their socks and where the rich went to buy their artichokes. So what have they done with it?'

My head bounced as I exhaled in derision.

'It's now going to become a car park and a shopping mall.' Spago shook his head in disbelief. 'And they had only just finished a car park and shopping mall the other side of town. How many car parks and malls do we need?'

Spago was one of the few people in the world who got better when he was self-righteous. Because although he was earnest he would also smile, like some people's stupidity amused him, and he wanted to amuse you too by showing what daft things they had done.

'I'm not against innovation,' he went on. 'I know we need investment, new enterprises and so on. But we can't just pour concrete everywhere. You remember that fiasco with Piazzale della Pace? For ages they had it fenced off whilst they debated who would get the contract to build a car park. And then some genius – I wish I knew who it was – simply said "no, let's just throw around some grass seed". And look at it now. It's one of the most beautiful squares in Italy. People go there to eat their sandwiches. Students sit around and sing songs at dusk. Couples court. Mothers take their children there to run around. There's our beautiful, bombed Palazzo della Pilotta, the statue of the partisan, there are those lights on the path that cuts from Via Garibaldi to the Palazzo, there are those clear pools of water. That's what attracts tourists, not somewhere to park their hire car, where a lift takes them to yet another expensive boutique. Cazzo!'

I nodded, smiling in agreement.

'Anyway,' he looked at me, 'you didn't ask me out to lunch to hear my philosophy of urban development.'

'No.' I looked at him apologetically. 'Although that's sort of what it's about.'

'Allora?'

'I'm on a case.'

'Always on a case, eh?'

I nodded and looked at him. 'Masi Costruzioni,' I said slowly.

He blinked slowly and stared at me. 'You really pick your cases.'

'What's that supposed to mean?'

'Masi?' He started shaking his head, keeping his eyes on me. 'Amedeo Masi?'

'What?'

'Put it this way: that guy's connected.'

'Meaning?'

He grunted. 'A few years ago traffic police stopped that senator from Italia Fiera, what's his name? Biondani, Biondelli or something. This guy's just about the most powerful person in the province. The leaves don't even fall from the trees unless he says so. Anyway, they stopped him for speeding and ran all the usual checks. You can imagine what he was like: spitting fire, threatening to sack all those honest, hard-working vigili because they had had the temerity to waylay their overlord. One of them takes objection and does his job properly. You know what they found? This senator is driving a car, a Mercedes convertible, registered to a company called Masi Costruzioni.'

'Huh.'

'Nothing came of it because there was nothing illegal going on. Masi came out and said the senator was an old friend of his, and that he often lends spare company cars to his closest friends. But it makes you wonder. What was Masi getting in return? He's a guy who's got his hands, as they say, in pasta.' Spago put his hand out palm down and rotated his fingers underneath his palm.

The waitress brought along a bottle, showed us the label and pulled off the cork. Spago tasted it and nodded.

'Go on,' I said as she walked away.

'Have a look online, I'm sure you'll find loads. Masi's not exactly been out of the news. There was a thing a few years ago when the Guardia di Finanza did some investigation into tax evasion. I can't remember what they called the operation. Pandora or Pegasus or something. Basically there are tax incentives for home-owners who do restoration work on historical properties. They get 36 per cent reduction on Irpef, something like that. So the Finanza could work out what companies were charging for restoration work from the tax incentives their clients were claiming, and could compare those charges to the earnings the companies were declaring on their tax returns. Guess what? Masi's company wasn't declaring the earnings. There was something like three million euros in unpaid taxes.'

'What happened?'

'What do you think? He spent a night in prison, was bailed, and within a few months there was a general amnesty passed. A useful condono for all those thieving constructors.'

'By who?'

'Which party passed the amnesty, you mean? Italia Fiera, who else?' He smiled, shrugging and shaking his head at the same time. 'Cazzo, if they gave me a three-million-euro rebate, I would happily spend a night in prison. From what I hear, prison in this country is like the golf course in America. It's where you make contacts and cut deals. If they give you three million for a night, I would stay for a month.' He was laughing now, raising his wine and talking loudly so that other people could hear. A couple turned round to look at him, smiling at his infectious chuckle.

'This guy,' I said, lowering my voice, 'this Masi. He's now building flats on land that someone was forced out of.'

'How do you mean?'

'A car has been burnt. Late-night calls. General intimidation.'

Spago was spinning the wine in his glass, making it fly up the sides so it almost came over the top. He watched it carefully and then let the liquid slow and settle. He took a sip and then leant towards me. 'They're building flats, eh? What was there before?'

'A prosciuttificio.'

'So the land has been reclassified?'

I nodded wearily.

'That's the way to make money.' He shook his head. 'If you know in advance what land is going to be reclassified you can make a mint.' He prodded an index finger on different parts of the table, like he was pointing out parts of the city where you could strike lucky. Then he looked up at me, nodding meaningfully. 'Say you've got ten biolche of agricultural land, it might be worth a few tonnes of wheat a year, a few thousand gallons of milk, whatever. But if it's residential, well, it could suddenly be worth millions. That's when the alchemy happens, when raw soil turns into gold. That's when the value of land jumps ten-fold. It's called cambio di destinazione d'uso.' He clicked the fingers of both hands and then fanned them through the air, thumbs leading the way, like he was a magician.

'Yeah, I heard. The guy who sold the prosciuttificio told me all about it. He's pretty sore about the whole thing.'

'I'm not surprised. If he hadn't been forced to sell he would have been sitting on a pot of gold. Who did he sell to?'

'A guy called Luciano Tosti.'

'Who sold to Masi?'

'Right. So I went to pay a visit to Tosti. I got an address for him out in Milan. Only when I get there I find he was killed a year ago.'

Spago whistled. The food arrived and we just stared at each other as the waitress put the plates in front of us.

Once she had retreated Spago leant closer. 'You know the difference between what Tosti bought it for and what he sold it for?'

I shrugged. 'I didn't ask. When I went to the Ufficio del Catasto I was only after a name.'

'The difference could be six figures. More. No doubt about it. Not bad money just for writing a cheque and biding your time. And he was working for Masi?'

I shrugged because I still didn't have proof. 'How would Masi know where to buy?' I asked. 'How would he know in advance which land was about to be declared residential?'

Spago rocked his head from side to side as if thinking about it. 'The most obvious candidate would be the city councillor for urban planning. What do they call that role? The assessore all'urbanistica, something like that. He's the guy who decides about the piano regolatore, the guy who decides about land usage.'

'I thought there was a commission . . .'

'Yeah, yeah, sure, there's a commission, and it does what the politicians tell it to. They're all political appointments anyway. How else do you think you get to sit on a commission?' He raised his eyebrows suggestively and put a large rectangular tortello in his mouth.

We ate in silence for a few minutes, each thinking about the tangled world of construction. The risotto was good, smooth and creamy but with a hint of grit in the rice and parmesan. Spago refilled our glasses.

'Knowing what land is going to be redesignated', he said, looking at me through the raised glass, 'is like knowing which numbers are going to come up in a lottery. I wouldn't mind knowing myself.'

'Yeah,' I said. 'The difference is you can't always buy that kind of lottery ticket. Sometimes people just don't want to sell the land you need, which is why cars get burnt and so on. They need a little bit of persuasion.'

'Do you know much about Masi's operation?' Spago asked.

I pulled out my phone and showed him the snapshot of the construction board: all the names of the architects and contractors and so on.

'You want to work through those,' Spago said, pointing at the phone screen with his fork. 'Because someone did Masi a favour when they tipped him off about the redesignated land, and you can be sure that he's repaying favours, putting work their way. Check out who got the big contracts, who the subcontractors are. That's the way it's always done in this business.'

'Meaning?'

'Completely legitimately. It's all above board, out in the open.'

'Sounds either honest or shameless.'

He smiled wearily. 'It's both. Who's the vending agent, by the way?'

'Some place called Casa dei Sogni.'

'Start there. That's the biggest racket there is. An agent takes 3 per cent on sale price, a bit from both ends. For doing what? Showing people around once or twice a day.' He was mopping up the butter with a bit of bread. 'Say they've got twenty-five flats to sell at 300 grand each.' He jabbed the wet bread in my direction. 'That agency's going to make a quarter of a million just for getting the contract. Anyone getting that kind of slice has got to be connected. It's not even corruption. Corruption doesn't mean anything to them. It's simply business. That's the way life is. Find out who runs that agency and I expect you'll find they've got a powerful relative or husband or something.' He put the bread in his mouth and looked over my shoulder and started talking almost to himself. 'That's why the family's such a strong institution in this country. It's not because of Catholicism. It's because money's got to go through a third person and who can you really trust to look after your money if you can't touch it yourself? It has to be family.'

He glanced at me to check I was listening. I was listening all right, but my head was spinning. I was already thinking about other things. He took a last swig of wine and wiped his mouth with the back of his hand.

'I've got to run,' he said. 'Thanks for lunch.' He stood up, but then bent back down and tapped a finger to his temple. 'Occhio, eh? These people sound serious.'

I nodded and watched him disappear. Only someone so idealistic could be so cynical, I thought, as he disappeared into the crowd of people at the bar. One or two slapped him on the back, shouting his name, as he went. He was that kind of person.

I stopped in a bar on Via Sauro to check where I was going. The barmaid was the typical simpaticona. Whilst I waited for her to notice me, I listened to her offering sighs and consolations for another customer. 'Ma cosa vuoi?' she kept saying to keep the conversation ticking over. The fourth or fifth time I heard her say it, I got in my order.

'Coffee.'

She went through the familiar motions – bashing the previous batch into a bin, refilling the thing, twisting it in place – whilst still listening to the man next to me grumbling about his son.

'You got a copy of *Tuttocasa*?' I said to her back when the man moved away.

'Outside in the rack,' she said over her shoulder.

I wandered outside and saw the familiar freesheets stacked in a white plastic rack. I took one, went back inside and sat on a barstool.

'Looking for a new place?' she asked, putting a red and white Lavazza tazzina in front of me.

The coffee was piping hot. I looked at her over the thick rim. She was already talking to someone else. I put the little cup down and opened up the yellow paper. It carried ads for all the houses and flats in vendita or affitto. There were pages and pages of mini paragraphs: descriptions of dream flats and houses in streets I had never heard of. It was clear we were in the midst of a crisis because almost every price said 'trattabile'.

Casa dei Sogni had a whole half-page ad. The name of the agency was written underneath a pediment supported by two neoclassical columns. It was on Via Garibaldi. I left a euro on the counter and headed over there.

A few minutes later I was standing outside an imposing building. Most estate agents' windows have pictures of the insides of apartments: slinky kitchens, a little bedroom, a few 'beams on view' as they say. This window was almost all made up of artist's impressions of what a finished block would look like. There were pictures of monolithic blocks with human dots in the foreground. There were photographs of 3D models with plastic trees. Casa dei Sogni was clearly into the wholesale market: not selling dinky little flats in the centro storico but new-builds in the suburbs. When the market was moving, they must have been making a mint.

Behind the prices, plans and photographs I could see a large, light office. Spotlights were suspended from taut, thin wires and the computer screens were as thin as coasters. There was a huge blow-up of an aerial photograph of the city.

The entrance was set back from the pavement, a glass and brass door behind an archway. When I walked in a young girl looked up.

'Buongiorno,' she said.

'Hi.'

She stood up, ready to do business. Like a lot of the office girls round here, she was showing more skin than clothing. 'Mi dica,' she said formally.

'I saw a new block of flats in Via Pordenone. Someone there said you're the vending agents.'

'Via Pordenone?' She sounded uncertain. 'Let me find the right folder.'

She turned round to the wall of fat files behind her. She put her head sideways to run her eyes across the names on the spines. I cocked my head in the same way, more to look at her than the folders.

'Ecco,' she said suddenly, reaching up on tiptoe and revealing the tanned small of her back. She brought the box folder over to a large, semicircular desk in the middle of the office and opened it up, pulling out plans and documents and the rest.

'Prego,' she said, pulling up a seat for me.

'Who's the builder?' I asked, wanting to make sure of the facts.

'Hang on,' she said, leafing through the papers. She made the usual sounds people make to fill the silence when they're looking for something. Two bars of tuneless singing. 'Here we go. Masi Costruzioni. One of the most reputable builders.'

'Are they all sold by now?'

'Only one of them, but we're doing viewings all the time. They're generating a great deal of interest.'

I've never met an estate agent who doesn't come out with that line. I looked at her with my chin on my chest and gave her a tired smile. 'Everything generates interest,' I said. 'It's generating money that's hard.'

'They go together. Money makes interest, and interest makes money.'

'What's the real situation?'

She lowered her voice, like she didn't want to admit it was slow. 'It's a far cry from what it was a year or two ago.'

'How do you mean?'

'Eh beh. There were three of us working here until recently. There was a queue of people snaking out the door. Now it's just me here and you're only the second or third person who's come in today.'

She was looking at a red elastic band that she was wrapping around her fingers.

'Don't get me wrong,' she looked up at me, trying to recover her professionalism, 'now's probably a good time to buy. You haven't got a lot of competition and you can negotiate pretty hard.'

'So you've only sold one so far?'

'Yeah. Sold one from the plans.'

'Like ordering a meal from a menu?'

'An expensive meal, mind.' She gave half a smile. 'I mean,' she corrected herself, 'in a way, it's a sensible way to purchase. It's cheaper to buy from the plans. If you were to buy now, before completion, you would certainly get a good deal.' She rummaged amongst the papers, fanning them out across the table until she found what she wanted. 'Here. You can get a three-bedroom flat, fourth floor, for three four nine. That's with a lift, cantina and garage. A two-bed for two nine nine.' She was about to unfold the plans and go back to selling mode.

'Which one has been sold?'

She shuffled the papers again. 'The penthouse.'

'You know who bought it?'

'Marina, I think. She often invests in the places we're selling. Says it reassures clients to know that the agent involved has also bought in the same block. It sends out the right message.'

'Who's Marina?'

She looked across at a thin flight of stairs at the back of the office and nodded. 'It's her agency.'

'And her surname's Casa dei Sogni?'

She smiled. 'Vanoli.'

'Marina Vanoli?' I said slowly. 'The name rings a bell.'

She opened her mouth and drew breath, like she was about to say something. But then she closed it and said nothing.

'Is she in?'

'She's upstairs.'

'Any chance I could have a chat with her?'

She nodded, stood up and walked off. I watched her go up the stairs and out of sight. I heard footsteps above my head. A few minutes later the girl came back down, followed by a woman who was wearing enough jewellery to rattle slightly as she walked. Her face looked like she had spent too much time and money trying to make herself beautiful and had gone beyond the point of no return, like eggs that have been beaten too long. Her cheeks were shiny and immobile, and she had bee-stung lips that looked about as soft as the sole of a shoe. Her neck, by contrast, looked about thirty years older than the rest of her.

At the bottom of the stairs she overtook her employee and walked towards me, hand outstretched. 'Marina Vanoli, piacere,' she said.

'Salve.'

'Come upstairs, we can talk there.'

I followed her back up the stairs and she led me through a heavy door into a sumptuous office: dark oil paintings and antiques in all directions, three sofas, a large plasma TV on the wall. I noticed the edges of the ceiling were curved rather than at right-angles, and there were faint, cracking frescoes all over it.

'Caffe?' There was a sharp, business-like tone to her voice.

'No.' I shook my head. 'Thank you.'

'Have a seat.' She motioned towards one of the old sofas. As I sat in it, it took my weight, the wide cushions slowly giving way until I almost sunk inside them. I tried to crab towards the left of the sofa to pull myself up on the arm. She sat on a black office chair holding a clipboard and a pen.

'Annalisa tells me you're interested in one of the new flats on Via Pordenone.'

'Very.'

'How can I help?' She tried to smile but her face was too rigid so she just bared her teeth.

'You bought one of those flats, right?'

'I did,' she purred. 'Amedeo Masi's the best constructor in this city. It was a great opportunity. Great location, great price. That whole area is . . .'

'Coming up?'

'Exactly.' She nodded eagerly.

'But it's between the motorway and the railway line.'

'Good transport links.' She tried to smile again, pleased with her translation.

'Did you buy it at market price?'

'That's the only price there is.'

'No discount?'

She frowned, not sure where the question was coming from. 'Market price,' she repeated like her mind was elsewhere. 'What's this all about?'

'Masi put the entire vending operation in your hands. That's quite a contract. Then I hear he's sold you the penthouse flat, the largest, lightest flat in the block.'

'Allora?'

'It makes me wonder what's going on.'

Her face was so rigid it was hard to read. Only her eyes seemed to move naturally and they were static, boring through me. 'What is it you want exactly?'

It sounded like she was opening negotiations.

'You ever heard of a man called Luciano Tosti?'

She shook her head, wobbling her wattles. I looked at her closely, but she stared back at me with a slight frown as if she really hadn't heard of him.

'Carlo Lombardi, how about him?'

Same face, same reaction. 'Who are these people?' She sounded impatient.

'How do you know Amedeo Masi?'

'He's a constructor. I'm an estate agent. Isn't it obvious?'

'Why did he choose you?'

'What do you mean?'

'Why did he ask you to sell his flats and not someone-else?'

She smiled and shrugged. 'I'm good at my job.'

She was so self-satisfied she didn't even seem to understand why I was asking the question. Didn't appear to understand that there was something unusual going on. Or if she did

84

understand, she had buried it deep under her own vanity, preferring to see herself rather than the secret.

Someone as hard-nosed as Masi didn't put that much work someone's way just because they're good at their job. It would have been cheaper for him to hire his own staff and set up an agency on his own. But he was giving a lucrative contract to Vanoli and it seemed a good guess that it was to thank someone for the tip-off about the redesignation of land. Vanoli, I suspected, was just a way to get money to someone else.

'Ci vediamo,' I said, trying to push my way out of the sofa.

She stood up and looked at me, bemused. She walked over to the door and held it open. 'Aren't you at least going to tell me what this is all about?' she said.

'I don't even know myself.'

I walked down the steps and nodded at the girl on the way out.

It was early evening now and the day was giving up the fight against darkness. I went over to Bragantini's factory. It was clear that the case was more serious than he or I had realised yesterday and I wanted to check he had organised some decent security. I pulled up at the factory and walked into reception. The receptionist was there with a different shade of spray-on clothes.

'You looking for Bragantini?' she asked.

I nodded and she got up to go and find him. I looked around the reception area. It was like any other: a couple of sofas, a low table with trade publications, a water cooler and a bin full of discarded plastic cups. I looked out of the window and could see the city on the other side of the river. I imagined it getting closer, moving nearer every minute.

'Prego,' said the receptionist at my back.

I turned round and saw the familiar scowl of Pino Bragantini. He looked tired.

'Did you sort out a security guard?' I asked.

'Sure,' he said. 'Let me introduce you.' He walked out into the car park and around to a side entrance. 'Tommy?' he shouted loudly. 'Tommy?'

We went inside. The corridor was narrow. There were doors off to the right into cramped storage rooms.

'Tommy,' Bragantini barked, pushing open the doors of each room.

A young black man emerged from a room further down the corridor. He didn't say anything but stood there eagerly.

'This is Tommy,' Bragantini said, holding his palm towards the boy.

We nodded at each other. I tried not to look unimpressed. He wasn't exactly the type of security guard I had had in mind. He was wearing an Inter Milan top. All immigrants knew that the fastest way to true integration was to adopt a local football team.

'You sleep here on site?' I asked.

'Won't get much sleep.' He smiled cheerfully. 'I'll get up every hour to check things.' He spoke Italian with a strong African accent, each sentence coming out breathily like he had been running hard.

'Seen anything?'

'Lot of wildlife.' He smiled again.

'You see anything, hear anything, you call me, OK?' I passed him a card.

'Sure.'

I looked at him again. He can't have been much more than sixteen or seventeen. He looked up from the card and nodded, eager to please.

Bragantini led me away, explaining that Tommy had been recommended to him by one of the men who worked in the factory.

'Not much of a security guard,' I said.

'What do you want? He's here at night and keeps an eye on things. What else do I need?'

I shrugged. 'You're sure he really is up at night and not just using your factory as a doss house? When I was that age I could sleep through a war.'

Bragantini threw his hands in the air to say he didn't know. 'He seems a good lad.'

'A good lad might not be enough against a bad man.'

Bragantini nodded wearily. 'Maybe you're right, but he's better than nothing.'

'And cheaper?'

He stopped walking and stared at me. 'I hired you to help me out, not to give me this sort of grief. I'm doing what I think is best. I'm trying to protect myself and my family. How many people do you think I can hire, eh?'

I gave way, looking at him and nodding like I agreed with him. 'You're right,' I said. 'I just want to make sure you've got the best protection possible . . .'

We were back outside now and he aimed his chin at the buildings I had been looking at before. 'I can feel them circling. Can feel the bastards coming after me. They're not brave enough to come and talk to me face to face like real men. They're just hiding out there somewhere, waiting for nightfall to come and attack.'

I didn't want to reassure him, to pretend that his car had been an isolated incident. He knew, instinctively, that he had been targeted, and we both knew there was more to come. It felt eerie standing there, staring at nothing but knowing they were readying themselves for the next attack. I felt powerless, unable to protect him, and I told him so.

He looked at me with unexpected melancholy. 'I don't think anyone can stop the spread of the city. If someone wants this land, they'll get it somehow, even if it means burying me under their concrete.'

We stared through the trees at the encroaching city. It felt like a vertical tidal wave that was about to crash down on us.

It was dark and cold by the time I got back to my place. I was walking towards my flat when I saw a young woman hanging around under the arches. She looked more like a young man from a distance: wide shoulders, short hair, but she was dressed elegantly, as if she had been out to dinner. She was looking around for someone, and it was obvious, when our eyes met, that I was the person. She smiled faintly from a distance and raised a hand as if I should recognise her. I did, but I wasn't sure where from.

'I'm sorry,' she said.

'What for?'

'Disturbing you.'

'Not at all.'

She looked at me and smiled bashfully. I looked at her more closely, but still couldn't place her. I must have seen her in another context but I couldn't work it out.

'I'm Amedeo Masi's daughter,' she said quietly, clearly seeing my confusion.

I nodded, recalling the young woman on the front desk at the man's office. She looked different now, dolled up for a night out but shivering slightly from the cold.

'You been waiting long?'

She smiled slightly. 'An hour or so.'

'Come on, come and have a drink.'

We walked towards the bar on the corner. She looked round as she went in, as if checking to see if there was anyone she knew.

'Soft or hard?' I asked her.

'Hard,' she said.

I got a couple of malts and we retreated to a table in the corner. It was a losco sort of bar: young men hanging around outside like they couldn't afford the drinks, but wanted to hear the music, or tap the passing trade, or try their luck with the women walking home.

'How did you find me?'

She reached into her handbag and pulled out one of my cards. I looked at her again: she had the same determined face as her father, a stare that told you she meant business.

'I know what you're trying to do,' she said with a trace of accusation in her voice.

'What's that?'

'You want to ruin my father.'

I laughed unintentionally and she looked at me fiercely. We sat there uneasily and stared at our drinks.

'I have no intention of ruining your father,' I said gently. 'I'm trying to solve a crime, nothing more.'

'He's committed no crime.'

'Maybe not, but the evidence doesn't look good.'

'The evidence?' She looked at me with disdain, shaking her head. 'You know nothing about it.'

'Isn't that why you came to see me, to put me right?'

She rolled her eyes, as if it were useless.

'I have nothing against your father. If anything, I rather admire him. But I'm trying to work out why his company is the beneficiary of these fires, and he hasn't explained himself.'

'Because he's too proud,' she shot back.

'Meaning?'

'He's too proud to admit to you what's really going on. He still thinks the company belongs to him, but it doesn't. His is just the name on the door.'

'What do you mean?'

She looked around before answering and then leant forward. 'A few years ago my father was the victim of fires just like the ones you're investigating. Car set alight at night, bricks thrown through the windows of the offices. Equipment stolen, stores burgled. It was happening once or twice a week.'

She was speaking quickly, with the same urgent passion as her father had. It was as if they both considered themselves misunderstood victims.

'Did they ever catch the vandals?' I asked.

'Of course not. But it wasn't just hooliganism. It felt co-ordinated, like someone was deliberately making trouble for us. Everything was happening all at once. Even reliable suppliers started messing us around, workers walked out, there were unannounced inspections. In the middle of it all, my father met a man who offered to sort everything out. Presented himself like some kind of troubleshooter, a fixer who could smooth out all the hassles. He was so desperate by then that he was ready to take any help going.'

'What kind of help was he offering?'

'He said he could step up security, that sort of thing.'

'Protection?'

'That wasn't the word he used, and my father didn't even

realise that's what was on offer. He just saw someone offering private security and he jumped at the chance.'

'What was the man's name?'

'Moroni. Giulio Moroni.'

I shrugged. The name meant nothing to me. 'Does he still work for your father?'

She sighed. 'It's more the other way round.'

'What do you mean?'

'It doesn't feel like my father's in charge any more. It's . . .' she twisted her head sideways and looked at the ceiling, 'it's like Moroni's taken over.'

'How?'

'I don't know. I don't understand it. It's like he's the boss.' She shook her head and corrected herself. 'He is the boss.'

It was a word that had echoes of the criminal underworld. I looked at her to see if her use of that word was casual, but she was nodding her head, sure of what she was saying. 'He pays all the workers in cash,' she said as if to underline the point. 'Pays everyone in cash. He's like a parasite gorging on my father's company, taking it over bit by bit.'

'And your father realises that?'

'He's in denial. Still pretends to himself that the company is his, that he's the man in charge.'

She put her head to one side, placed an index finger inside her fringe and pushed the short hair from her forehead. She looked at me meaningfully, though I wasn't sure what she meant. I assumed she wanted my help in ridding her father's company of the unwanted Moroni. She had come here in the dark and cold to tell me the lie of the land, and now she wanted me to do something about it.

'Where's your father now?' I asked.

'Why?' She frowned.

'I'll talk to him before I talk to Moroni. Where is he? At home?'

She stared at me like I had disappointed her. 'He'll be asleep.'

'Then I'll wake him up.'

She was shaking her head. 'Don't tell him I spoke to you.'

'Where is he?'

She sighed, staring blankly at the table as if she thought she had made a mistake. 'At home. Via Solferino.'

'What number?'

'37.'

We stared at each other for an instant. I remembered her saying she lived with her father, so I offered to drop her back. She said she would walk. Said it like it was an expression of independence or disappointment or something. It was late by now, so I offered again and she stared at me, her face changing as she did so. She seemed to let go of some tension. It looked as if she were about to break down and she looked away, biting her lower lip. We sat like that for a few minutes.

'It'll be all right,' I said quietly as she blew her nose.

She sighed again, shaking her head. 'My father gets accused of everything. His name is only ever in the papers when he's suspected of corruption or whatever. And every time it's nothing to do with him. It's like Moroni makes the money and my father takes the blame. That's why when you came in this morning, and I heard you talking about arson attacks, I just knew it was to do with Moroni. That's the way he works.'

'Where does he operate from, this Moroni?'

'He works out of a portakabin in Via Pordenone.'

'He's the one I met this morning? The foreman?'

'That's him. Some foreman,' she spat with contempt.

We walked to my car and drove through the city in silence. I parked outside the block and opened my door, but she sat where she was, not moving.

'Allora?' I said.

'If we come in together he'll know it was me that told you. I'll just sit here and listen to the radio for a while.' She saw me looking at her. 'If that's OK,' she said.

'You sure?'

She nodded.

I left her the keys, walked up to the front of the house and rang the bell. There were no lights on and I assumed Masi must have gone to bed already. I held the buzzer again, pushing it harder than necessary so that the end of my finger went white.

'Chi è?' said a sleepy, irritated female voice.

'My name's Castagnetti. I'm looking for Masi.'

The line went dead. A minute later he picked up. 'Chi è?'

'Let me in. I want to know about Giulio Moroni.'

There was silence and then he clicked me in. He was standing there in a dressing gown, looking smaller somehow. His gingerish hair was all ruffled. He snarled and nodded his head to the right. I followed him into an ornate room crammed with cheap antiques: semicircular lampshades on top of woodworm-eaten lamps. On the walls were imposing, gold-framed pictures of women looking wanly upwards. The domed ceiling had crumbling cherubs, the twirling garlands losing their gold-leaf. A black spider's thread hung from the ceiling, wafting left and right. A forest of photo frames was reclining on a chest of drawers.

He stood in the centre of the room, his fists in his dressing-gown pockets.

'Tell me about Giulio Moroni,' I said.

He shot me a stare as if I had just named his wife's lover. He was about to say something, but then put his mouth back together.

'Go on,' I nudged.

'What about him?'

'I heard he's the real power behind the throne. He's the one who really controls your company.'

'Who told you that?'

'I hear all your suppliers get paid in cash straight from Moroni's personal safe.'

'He deals with invoices, certainly. That's his job.'

'In cash?'

'I don't know how he pays them.'

'How do you pay him?'

'Eh?' He was stalling.

'He pays your workers,' I said. 'Pays all the electricians and plumbers and plasterers and carpenters. So you and your company end up having to reimburse a lot of money. So how do you reimburse him?'

He stared at me, snarling and breathing heavily. 'Why do you want to know about Giulio Moroni?'

'I'm investigating a case of arson. I told you that this morning.'

'Why do you think he's got anything to do with it?'

I lowered my chin and looked at him as if to tell him I wasn't stupid.

He growled and shook his head. 'He gets the end product.'

'Meaning?'

'Units.'

'What units?'

'Flats.'

I frowned and Masi looked at me like maybe I was stupid. 'He wanted to buy up what we were building,' he said. 'Offered to pay for them in advance. Pay wages, suppliers and so on out of his own pocket as a down-payment on the flats of the future. It all sounded perfectly reasonable at first. It meant I couldn't lose. It meant I wasn't having to go to banks for loans and that I had guaranteed sales at the end.' He put his chin on his shoulder, staring down to the right and smiling bitterly at the memory. 'It was too good to be true.'

'It wasn't true?

He rolled his eyes. 'It was true all right. He paid suppliers and he got the flats. It's just that what seemed perfect to start with became something else altogether. I thought it meant I couldn't lose. What it really meant was I couldn't win. I didn't even need to be there any more. It was like he had become the company, he was running the whole operation. Sometimes a project would take eighteen months from plans to completion, and all I would have left to show for it were a couple of flats. The rest were his.'

'A couple of flats?' I repeated. 'That's an OK profit for eighteen months.'

He shook his head impatiently. 'That's not the point.'

'I thought profit was always the point.'

'You thought wrong.' He stared at me. 'There are many things more important than profit. If you lose money one year, you can find it the next. But lose your reputation, you might never get it back. I care about my name, about the name I pass on to my children and they pass on to theirs.'

'What's wrong with your name?'

He stared at me with anger for my faked naivety. 'You know full well. Everyone repeats the same bull. About my links to politicians, allegations of corruption and so on. You knew all about my reputation before you met me. You had already judged me before you set eyes on me.'

It was true. I had heard the usual gossip and had assumed the worst. I wasn't sure if Masi was really the victim in all this, or if he was just good at playing the victim. But for the first time I felt sorry for him. I didn't need him to spell out what was happening in his company. He had accepted protection from the worst kind of person and had ended up becoming just a figurehead, a front for a sophisticated mechanism to turn cash into accommodation. Masi had become little more than a launderette for dirty money.

'Where does he get all his cash?' I asked.

He shrugged, closing his eyes and shaking his head. 'I don't ask, but I can guess.'

'What kind of sums?'

'The costs of building a block of flats run into the millions. Every payment he makes is in cash.' He paused, to check I was listening. 'And we build more than one block a year.'

'That's a lot of paper.'

We looked at each other as if we were about to seal some sort of alliance.

'You want shot of him?'

He snorted derisively. 'I don't think it's that easy.'

'Just tell me what I need to know. Who decided that the contract to sell the flats in Via Pordenone should be given to Marina Vanoli?'

His barrel chest rose and fell as he prepared to betray his enemy. 'He did.'

'He who? Moroni?'

'Sure.'

'Do you know why?'

He didn't even reply, just flashed me a false smile.

'You mean Moroni was thanking his political contacts?'

'Something like that.'

'And that case a few years ago of one of your company cars being driven by a senator.' He snarled at the memory. 'That was Moroni too was it?'

'I didn't even know the senator. I've never had anything to do with politicians. And then suddenly I see my name being dragged through the mud as if I had been paying bribes all my professional life.'

'Didn't you confront Moroni about it?'

'It was the first time I realised quite who I was dealing with. He said things to me then that I've never forgotten.'

'Like what?'

'Told me what would happen if I ever interfered in his business.'

'His business?'

'That's what it was by then.' He was staring into the distance, focusing on nothing but his own demise.

'And what did he say would happen?'

'You can guess,' he said, still staring into the abyss.

I looked at him. He was his old, abrasive self, but he looked tired and defeated, as if he had finally confessed to himself that he was no longer in charge. His secret was out.

'So you let it lie, let him take over the business?'

'It was booming,' he said quickly. 'We were flying. Every time something went out to tender, we won the contract. Why wouldn't I let it lie?'

'Did you ask yourself why you were winning contracts?'

'It was obvious. The company was looking after the right people.'

'Meaning?'

'Politicians are always thirsty.'

'And you were quenching their thirst?'

'Eh?'

'You said they were always thirsty. You were buying them drinks so to speak?'

He stared at me through a frown. 'I don't know any politicians. Not one. I've never been someone who moves in the right salons. But Moroni did. Knew everyone. He used to say that you can't build a sandcastle in this city unless you contribute to politicians.'

'In return for what?'

'For goodwill, a kindly disposition,' he said, lowering his voice. 'Don't pretend you don't know how it is. We needed work, planning permission, building permits. They needed funds to fight elections. We helped each other out. That's democracy.'

'Sort of.'

'That's how it works in this country. Always has and always will.'

I shrugged, like I wasn't sure.

'That's how it is, believe me.'

'I thought all that stopped with Tangentopoli.'

He snorted. 'That's the biggest charade this country has ever seen. Contagious self-righteousness, an acute case of the indignations. It happens every two or three decades or so, makes people feel better about themselves. Then it goes back to how it was before. Maybe different methods, but basically just the same. If you want a contract you've got to grease it, believe me.'

'And how did Moroni grease it?'

'The usual. Asked a politician if they knew any electricians. So we employed the person they recommended. Asked them to recommend an architect, and they had someone in mind. Always the same story. Overpriced and incompetent. We were employing people who barely knew their left from their right. Half the time we had to employ a second workman to correct what they had done wrong. But that's the way it worked. We just kept employing their friends and family and they kept giving us the permits. Mutual back-scratching, that's all.'

'Is that what happened to Luciano Tosti as well?'

'Eh?'

'Luciano Tosti.'

He frowned and looked cross, like he didn't enjoy wasting time on incomprehension. 'Who's that?'

'He's the person who bought the prosciuttificio on Via Pordenone. You bought the place from him a few months later.'

'What about him?'

'He was murdered.'

I watched him closely. For all his faults, Masi was an honest man. He didn't fake shock and horror, but nodded slowly with his eyes closed.

'I heard,' he said.

'You knew about it?'

'Of course I did. The Carabinieri were round here within days. They were investigating his finances and that led them here. Sure, I knew about it.'

'And?'

'And what?'

'You thought Moroni was responsible?'

He stared at me. 'Tosti was stupid.'

'What's that supposed to mean?'

'He was supposed to sit on that land for six months. Nothing else. He was given the money to buy it and was then supposed to sell it on. But once he realised what was up, that the land was reclassified as residential, he saw his chance. He didn't sell it on. Started demanding this and that, offering it round to other constructors.'

'And Moroni wasn't happy?'

'That's an understatement. He said people like Tosti were only good for foundations.'

'Nice.'

'He meant it.' He looked at me to check I understood how serious he was.

'You think Moroni was involved in his death?'

'Wouldn't you?' he said sharply.

'Did the Carabinieri question him?'

'I don't think so. They didn't even know who he was. Even if they had come across him, they would have thought he was just some foreman.'

I heard the front door click open and the man's daughter came in. Her father asked where she had been as if she were a teenager and she smiled and kissed him on the cheek. As she walked past me we shook hands briefly and she surreptitiously gave me my car keys.

'Where does he live?' I asked Masi.

'Who? Moroni?'

I nodded.

'Just round the corner. That's the rub. I even see him when I go out for a walk.'

'Which street?'

'Duca Alessandro. It's number 57. One of those beautiful old villas.' He looked at me with a weary expression. 'Mind if I go back to bed now?'

'Prego.'

He let me out and I walked round to Via Duca Alessandro. I found the villa at 57 and saw a light on on the ground floor. When I buzzed, a voice came on the line almost immediately like he was used to having visits at this time of night.

Moroni stood by the door as I came in. He was fully dressed still and had his glasses on. His face looked saggy like some kind of dangerous dog whose viciousness was disguised behind wrinkles. At his back I could see a desk with a long, horizontal green light on it.

'You again?' He looked over his half-moon glasses at me. 'Did you buy a flat?'

I passed him a card between my fingers. He took it, looking at me before he read it. When he looked back up at me his face was changed. It looked cold and dead somehow. He didn't say anything.

'Mind if I ask you a couple of questions?'

He walked to his desk without replying. I watched him stand behind it like it was some kind of shield.

'What exactly do you want to know?' The words were spoken so slowly that he sounded both bored and threatening.

'I hear you always buy in cash.'

He looked up briefly at the ceiling. 'I work in construction. Cash is king. There's no other currency in this business.'

'And where does your cash come from?'

'A cashpoint.' He was looking at me with a 'screw you' face. 'If you're interested in my career, I can send you a curriculum vitae.'

'I'm not interested in the official version.'

'That's the only version there is.' He put out a hand towards a chair and nodded. He sat down himself and his tone seemed to become more warm. 'Listen, in this line of work it's hard to get the right labourers. You pay people in cash they come back for more. It makes them punctual, polite. Not virtues to be taken for granted. Everybody is happy.'

'Except the taxman.'

He rolled his head. 'Whether they pay taxes or not isn't my concern. Every construction company does it.'

'Doesn't make it right,' I said.

'What's right?' he asked, smiling at me with a sneer.

'Try lawful.'

'Ah, the law,' he said, throwing his hands in the air as if we were talking about something ethereal, a fantasy of men's imaginations.

He was one of those men who thought that the law was the enemy and that infringement of it was a form of self-defence. He didn't care what the law was, as long as it didn't come after him. He was like a lot of people: those who thought that the further you could get from the law the better. It meant you were more independent and brave, somehow more manly.

'What about Luciano Tosti?'

'Who?' he barked back quickly.

'He bought the prosciuttificio in Via Pordenone where you're now building your beautiful flats. Then he sold it on to

Masi Costruzioni. He was put up to it by someone who had inside information about future building permits.'

He was staring at the desk like he was wondering what to do with me.

'Luciano Tosti was murdered,' I said, watching him closely.

He nodded slowly and then fixed me with his lazy eyes again. 'I know,' he said.

'How did you find out?'

'I heard that Masi was talking to the Carabinieri and I found out why.'

'You don't like Masi talking to the Carabinieri?'

He shot me a stare. 'What exactly is it you want?'

'I want to find out who's been lighting fires around town. And now I'm on it, I'm kind of getting interested in what happened to Tosti.'

'Talk to Masi,' he said.

'I have.'

'And he told you to come to me?'

I didn't know what to say. I tried to think of some way of defending Masi from the notion that he had led me to Moroni, but nothing came to me. Moroni smiled and nodded his head.

'He thinks I'm involved does he?' He said it like he would settle the score in his own time.

'He didn't even mention you,' I said quickly.

'So what brings you here?' He narrowed his eyes. I shrugged weakly and he started to laugh. 'You think you're smart, eh?'

'I think you are.'

He picked up my card and looked at it again. He held it with his thumb and forefinger as if he were holding unpleasant rubbish and opened a drawer. He dropped the card inside the drawer and shut it again.

'Why would you want to do your work? Sneaking around at night, prying into people's lives?'

'I like to see safe streets. Like to see criminals inside.' I stared at him.

He smiled without showing his teeth. 'I'm a businessman,' he said.

'That's a big word. You run a launderette. You use Masi's company to clean your cash.'

'Why don't you tell me exactly what you're accusing me of and I'll tell you how I plead?' The man was almost more unsettling when he adopted such a hospitable tone.

I stared at him, disconcerted by his lazy stare. 'You've been getting tip-offs about what land is about to be flipped from agricultural to residential and have been commissioning thugs to force people off their land.'

He laughed openly, like he was genuinely amused. 'Innocent.'

'You put Tosti up to buying Lombardi's prosciuttificio and when he didn't sell on to you at the agreed price, you put a price on his head.'

He laughed again, before leaning forward and suddenly dropping the smile. 'Innocent. I'm a businessman. I buy and sell. I hire and fire. That's it.'

'Hire and fire? You fired Tosti all right.'

He was shaking his head.

'I met Tosti's widow. She's got a lot of money in the bank and wants to buy a slice of justice for her dead husband. I thought you might want to sell some information.'

107

'Sure,' he said sarcastically. 'I don't know anything about his murder. Wish I did, because I would punish the idiot who whacked him.'

It was the first time he had said something unexpected. 'Why?'

'Because Tosti went to his grave owing me money. And he's not going to give it back now, is he?'

'Tosti's gone, but his money isn't. I told you. His widow's sitting on it, and she's more concerned about justice than her bank balance.'

'Yeah, well, like I told you, I don't know anything about it.' He stared at me over the top of his glasses. It felt as if he was being sincere for the first time, trying to underline the fact that he was telling the truth.

'Why do you say he owed you money?'

'Because he did.'

'Why?'

He didn't say it, but I knew. And he knew I knew. He had arranged for Tosti to take possession of the prosciuttificio and had expected it to be sold on for a certain price. Tosti had bounced the price and Moroni felt he was still owed.

'Listen,' he said, trying to contort his weary face into a friendly pose, 'why don't you come and work for me? I could pay you double what you're on now. Give you top-end work. Surveillance stuff in Rome. Go after the real criminals. I can line up for you the kind of investigations that could make your name on a national level.'

I smiled in derision. 'I thought you were just a foreman.'

His face found its cold sneer again. 'Think about it.'

'I already have. And I've already got a client.'

'Who?'

'Pino Bragantini. His car was burnt a couple of nights ago.'

He laughed like he was genuinely amused about something. 'You better get to work then.' He stood up and went over to the door, holding it open for me. 'Buonanotte,' he said with sarcastic courtesy.

It was the middle of the night when the phone went. I knew it was trouble as soon as the desperate, digital ringing woke me up.

'Sì,' I said.

'The factory's on fire.' It was Bragantini. His voice sounded frantic. 'The whole thing's up in flames. The whole lot.' I could hear a roar in the background, like he was in a forest of falling trees.

'Have you called the fire brigade?'

'Yes, yes. But I can't see him. I can't see him anywhere.'

'Who?'

'Tommy. I can't see him.'

'Who's Tommy?'

'He's the security boy you told me to get in. He's sleeping in there tonight. Like you said he should.'

In his desperation he was putting it all on me. Like it was my idea and so now it was my fault. I told him I would be round there immediately.

I got dressed in a hurry and ran downstairs. Long before I got there I saw the orange tongues in the distance lighting up the night sky. As I got closer I could see the revolving lights of the emergency services and the silver arcs of water aimed at the angry fire. It looked hopeless. Men in hi-viz tops were running around the building, shouting to each other.

Eventually I worked out what they were shouting: 'Tommy Mbora. Tommy Mbora'. The flames were completely out of control, leering at us from every window, dancing in parallel lines to taunt our impotence. The noise was deafening.

Bragantini ran up to me. His eyes were so wide he looked like someone from a cartoon whose neck had been squeezed. 'They can't find him,' he screamed, leaning closer to me so that I could hear. 'No one's seen him.'

'He's definitely in there?'

'I assume so. You saw where he slept.'

'In that corridor?'

'Right. One of those rooms.'

'Where is it?'

He threw his palm in the air in the direction of the fire. It was a furious gesture, as if to say it made no difference.

We could do nothing other than watch. The flames eventually died for lack of fuel, but it took a few hours during which they came and went, disappearing from one window to reappear at another. Officials kept coming up to Bragantini to talk to him, taking notes. He called a lawyer, who arrived as it was getting light. By then the flames had been replaced by a smouldering, spitting blackness. The birds were singing as if nothing had happened, chirping away like it was another normal day.

It was a cold spring morning, blissfully still now. The grass had a sheen of dew and webs. Tall trees looked majestically static. The mist was lifting and the sky was going from white to blue. I walked around the site, staring at the ground. There were clumps of white foam everywhere like patches of melting snow. A lot of litter: cigarette butts, an old shoe, a chocolate bar wrapper, the rectangular plastic packaging for tissues. I walked around for half an hour. Head down, trying to find anything useful.

Looking for evidence is like looking for a queen on the frames of the bee hive. Every time you look at bees you keep an eye out for the queen, hidden amongst the tens of thousands of other black-brown dots, amongst the workers and drones. You see the colony crawling all over the brood, all over each other, and almost hypnotise yourself to find that one elusive queen. Sometimes people put a dot on her back, but even then she's hard to find. You have to lift frame after frame, turn them over, watch the edges and corners. You concentrate but sort of switch off at the same time. I was doing the same now. Looking for something different. Something that was hidden, camouflaged amidst everything that was similar, but out there somewhere.

I put everything I found in a plastic bag. If none of it was important, at least I had tidied up the countryside. I went over to the river and watched the water. The sound of it was soothing after the aggressive heat of the night. I stood there staring at the cool water, amazed that nature could be so beautifully oblivious to human stupidity.

Walking back towards the shell of the factory, I saw two people carrying a stretcher. They were wearing the orange uniforms of the assistenza pubblica. It looked like they were carrying a burnt log or beam. They placed the stretcher on the ground and I approached, seeing the long black form from between their legs: you could barely tell it was once human. It stank of scorched meat. I could hear a voice talking about dental records.

'That Tommy?' I said like I knew him.

They turned round to look at me, making space. I took a closer look and almost gagged on the putrid stench of damp, burnt flesh. There was nothing left of him. No hair, no skin, just a lipless grimace and flesh clinging to bone like a bin-liner to a lamp-post.

I turned away and saw the jawline from the fire station. He was even taller, more chiselled, in his helmet and uniform. He nodded when he saw me walking towards him.

'Deliberate?' I asked straight up.

He nodded his head to one side, a non-committal 'probably'. 'There's shattered glass from the windows on the inside of the building.'

'Smashed from the outside?'

'Looks that way. And no smoke on the underside of the glass which means the glass was shattered prior to the fire.'

'Deliberate,' I said conclusively.

He rocked his helmet from side to side, still not prepared to commit.

'Was there an accelerant?'

'Almost certainly.' He closed his eyes at the same time as if it were the only way to keep his anger from spilling over.

'Which was?'

'The usual.' His eyes opened and stared down at me.

'Petrol?'

'Right.'

'Arson then?'

He opened his hands like he still wasn't prepared to be conclusive. We stared at each other for a second, like we were sealing a pact. Then I thanked him and moved away.

I spent the morning going round all the petrol stations in the city. The Agip ones were easily recognisable, all the same: each forecourt had the same square red columns supporting a yellow and white roof. At each one the same symbol of a six-legged animal breathing red fire on its tail. Every word written was in lower-case letters with double red lines: aperto, cassa, centro gomme.

Most people were more interested in my card than my questions. Many just shrugged, said they had no recollection of anyone filling up a petrol can in the last week or two. Most of them only worked shifts anyway, so told me to come back at other times when someone else might be able to help.

It must have been about the eighth or ninth filling station that something came up. As usual I had had to wait until the customers were done. This time I enjoyed the wait. The girl behind the counter had short blond hair and bee-stung lips. She looked tough and beautiful at the same time, even with her red, silver and yellow Agip outfit on.

I watched the forecourt whilst she served customers. There was an old beaten-up van there with nothing written on it except, by hand, 'no logo vintage'. Old men walking home with their shopping took shortcuts across the forecourt. On the far side was a yellow caritas bin for used clothes and shoes and beyond that the car-wash with its furry, coloured columns spiralling upwards like a Twister lollipop.

'Can I help?' she said when there was no one left in her little booth.

I put my card on the counter. She picked it up and read it. 'What kind of investigator?'

'Anything. Mind if I ask you a couple of questions?'

She looked at me like she was preparing her defence. 'Go on.'

'I'm looking into an arson attack, trying to trace someone who might have bought a can or two of petrol recently from a station somewhere in the city . . .'

She nodded, staring at me with green eyes. She was even more beautiful close up. She looked young but had the kind of face that said she had suffered and survived. 'People usually don't buy cans of petrol at this time of year,' she said.

'Why not?'

'They usually buy them in the late spring, summer. You know, when they need petrol for their mowers, or when they want a spare can in the back of the car for going on holiday.'

'So you haven't seen anyone?'

'That's what I'm saying. I noticed it because it's unusual at this time of year. A guy came round last night. Came in twice. Once to buy the cans, then to pay for the juice.'

'Remember the car?'

She looked at the ceiling and shook her head.

'Remember him?'

She stared into the distance for a couple of seconds and did a slow-motion shrug. 'Youngish. Thirty, I suppose. Round face, thinning hair. He looked, I don't know, a bit like a loser. Like he was a bit sad.'

'Would you recognise him if . . .'

'If I saw him again? Sure. I would have thought so.'

'Can you show me the can he bought?'

She came round the front and walked to one side of her booth. She pointed at a green five-litre can. 'He bought two of those.'

'Got a till receipt?'

'Should do. I could work out how much it was. Two cans, five litres of petrol in each. I think he paid cash though.'

'And you've got CCTV?'

'You want to see yourself on television?' She pointed at the grey screen by her till. I leant forward and caught a glimpse of my short hair leaning forward.

'And it records onto tape?'

'All digital now,' she laughed at the idea of tape. 'Gets stored on a hard-drive.'

'So in theory the man's mug is in there somewhere?'

'Should be.'

'You want to look for it?'

'I'm kind of busy at the moment.'

'And you work here full-time?'

'For the moment.'

'Thinking of leaving?'

'I'm not going to work here for the rest of my life.'

I looked at her, not sure if I was excited because I had a lead or because she was it. 'What's your name?'

'Gaia.'

'You got anyone who can stand in for you for a couple of hours?'

'Why?'

'To go look for this guy. I've got an idea where he might show up.'

'Hang on.' She reached for the phone and dialled. I listened to her conversation: 'Any chance you can cover for me for a couple of hours? Something's come up.' She was listening and nodding. 'I know, I know, thank you,' she said and hung up. 'He'll be here in five minutes.'

'I'll wait for you in my car.' I pointed at the vehicle.

'No offence,' she said bashfully. 'But I don't get into cars with complete strangers. You say', she looked at my card, 'you're a private investigator. You got anyone who can vouch for you?'

I gave her Dall'Aglio's number in the Questura. He wasn't exactly well disposed towards me, but he knew I didn't take young girls for a ride without a good reason. She was picking up the phone again as I walked out.

A few minutes later a man went into the office. Gaia came out and opened the passenger door. She sat down next to me and smiled. 'You want to know what your friend the Carabiniere said?'

'He's not exactly a friend.'

'He told me you're a maverick and a loner.' She was looking at me and smiling. 'But that I would be fine with you. What makes you a maverick?'

I shrugged and started the engine. 'I do things my way. I don't have a uniform or an operating manual. That makes Dall'Aglio think I'm dangerous.'

I could feel her looking at me as I pulled out and it made me uncomfortable. 'What's this about?' she asked.

'The man who bought those cans last night set fire to a factory. The fire killed a man. I've got an idea where he might show up,' I said.

'So? What do you want me to do?'

'Sit in this car with a pair of binoculars for a few hours, watching who goes in and who comes out.'

'OK,' she said breezily.

We headed towards Via Pordenone, to the place where Lombardi used to have his prosciutto place. It was likely there would be more workmen coming and going there than at the Masi offices. And if Moroni really was the brains behind the scam, that's where the action would be.

It took a while to get there and I could still feel her watching me. We parked on the other side of the road, about fifty metres back from the portakabin and the entrance to the site. I passed her the binoculars and told her to watch for the man.

She laughed quietly to herself.

'What?' I asked.

'It's just funny. I've never been on a date like this.'

I turned to look at her, but she had the binoculars to her eyes and was facing forwards. Now she had taken off her uniform she looked even better. She was wearing tight jeans and a T-shirt which looked a size or two too small. It didn't look like she had brushed her short blond hair for weeks. It was slightly curly. There was something about her that looked less manicured than most women round here and I liked her for it.

'So how did you get into this game?' She looked at me briefly.

'Same as everyone else.'

'Which is?'

'Infidelity investigations. Almost everyone I know in this line started out checking up on errant spouses. It's like the gutter work of the profession.'

'You serious?'

'Sure. There are thousands of people out there who want someone to check up on their wife or their husband. Thousands and thousands. They pay good money for you to tail them. It's easy work and easy money.'

She gave a non-committal grunt, sounding unimpressed.

'Infidelity is like the apprenticeship. A lot of privates are ex-police or services. That or techno wizards. But most I know came up the same way as me, putting the final nail in the coffin of matrimonial bliss.'

'Must make you pretty cynical about romance?'

'Doesn't take much to make me cynical.'

She kept staring ahead, but then suddenly put the binoculars the other way round and turned them on me. 'Does it take much to make you romantic?'

'I wouldn't know.'

'Why not?'

I shrugged. I wanted to change the subject. 'Seen anything?'

She put the binos back the right way and looked over towards the portakabin. 'Nothing. You're avoiding my question.'

'I can't remember what it was.'

'It was about why you wouldn't know about romance.'

'Yeah well.'

'Yeah well,' she repeated. 'On most first dates men pretend to be all romantic and get less so each time you see them. At least you're cold from the start.' She chuckled gently, like it was more compliment than criticism.

'I've spent a lifetime trying not to thaw.'

'Meaning?'

I didn't want to go into it all. About losing my parents and all that bullshit. Whenever I go there, people start being sympathetic, wanting to hug me or mother me. They want to make up for it, like they ever could.

'Forget it,' I said.

'OK,' she said simply, without offence.

We sat there like that for a few minutes. Her watching the car park, me staring out of the window, wondering about her. There was a tense silence in the car now. Partly because we were there on the sly, but mainly because we were sitting together, two strangers, each one of us not looking at the other but hearing the other's breathing, sensing the other's electric presence.

'How about you?' I said eventually.

She told me everything from start to finish. Gave me a whole biography in a few minutes. How she had lost her mother in a car crash, how her father had brought her up on his own. The petrol station was his little kingdom, and that's why she worked there, even though she longed to do something else. She wanted to keep him company, help him out. As she was talking I watched her, feeling an unexpected desire to tell her about the symmetry to our lives.

'That's how I lost mine too,' I said when she had finished.

'What?'

'My parents. They died in a car crash too.'

Now she stared at me properly, searching my face. 'Merda,' was all she said. No false sympathy, just 'merda'. I liked her for it.

We didn't talk much after that but the tension was gone. It was like we had found what we had in common and were comfortable. We were united by something so deep that there wasn't any embarrassment. She just kept looking for the loser with the petrol cans.

We were there for two hours in intimate silence. I listened to the sound of hammering and of falling gravel. I tried to read the letters on the huge white funnels of intonaci and malti. I looked at everything on the site: people had written the names of their favourite football teams on the thick planks upended like skirting boards around the scaffolding. There was a perforated orange sheeting wrapped around poles weighed down by sandbags. Concrete slabs and cigarette butts were strewn across the cracking mud. Film-wrapped bricks sat on pallets. Everywhere there were signs in yellow triangles: a black exclamation mark, a helmet. Weeds were already pushing up through the mud. There were neat hillocks of gravel, sodden cardboard boxes, a broken filing cabinet, a solitary bath, one hubcap, a fire extinguisher, long coils of plastic hose. Thick, ribbed plastic tubes poked out of the mud like science fiction plants growing in the ground. There were saplings amongst the dandelions.

In the end we gave up waiting for the man who had filled up the night before. It had been a long shot anyway and I apologised for wasting her time.

'Sometimes you expect a connection and it just doesn't come,' I said.

'I felt a connection,' she said, looking at me.

I laughed self-consciously. 'Me too.'

I drove her back to the petrol station. 'You'll look through the CCTV footage and find him?'

'As soon as I get off work.'

'Give me a call,' I said.

She nodded, holding my stare like there was more to say. Then she patted the top of the car and walked back to her booth.

I headed towards the city. I parked the car at home and walked into town through the oldest quarter. The thin houses, three or four storeys high, looked like books on a shelf, all at different heights, and none of them properly vertical any more. They looked timeless but for the aerials and satellite dishes on their tiled roofs. I looked up and saw the swallows soaring and diving in the sky. I could see an old woman leaning out of her window to pull the washing line towards her as the rain began coming down. The pulleys squeaked as the large clothes crabbed closer to her.

As I came up Via Saffi towards Via della Repubblica, I saw a demonstration heading towards the piazza. There were people holding candles and flags and blowing whistles.

Getting closer I could make out the familiar logos of various left-wing parties on the flags and the acronyms of the three main unions. Many had new-looking banners with, in identical style, one word: Basta.

'What's going on?' I asked one earnest-looking boy who was trying to walk without the wind putting out his candle.

'We're holding a vigil in the piazza.'

'What for?'

'There's been another white death.'

Anything white is supposed to be innocent. A 'white voice' is a boy's voice before it breaks. A dead child is always given a white coffin. And a 'white death' is an accidental death, a tragedy that happens in the workplace.

'You mean Bragantini's factory?' I asked him.

'That's right.' He walked on, holding the candle like it was a new-born chick that he didn't want to drop. 'A young immigrant was burnt alive there last night.'

I followed the corteo as far as the piazza. They were mostly students and a few old crusaders. There wasn't the usual stage, but someone had a megaphone that was being passed around so that people could broadcast their indignation. They kept saying 'basta'. Enough white deaths. Enough workplace slaughter. They pulled out all the usual rhetorical stops, talking about resistenza and ingiustizia, talking about contempt for the padroni and solidarity with the workers. There wasn't a worker amongst them by the looks of it.

I watched it all with an air of detachment. People always seem to be longing for an excuse to get indignant. It's like they're almost grateful for another injustice which allows them to wring their hands. They identify with it because it underlines their belief that they themselves are the exploited, abused victims of some timeless oppression. That feeling lends an edge of anger to their indignation, and tinges their noble solidarity with personal pain. As usual, I felt that these left-wing parties had their hearts in the right place, but that they had it all wrong. They didn't understand what had happened, or what was going on.

More people were arriving now, some waving flags saying 'Bragantini Assassino', others cheerfully blowing whistles like they were at some Brazilian carnival. It was like they were happy they finally had something to shout about. A few old-fashioned red flags with a hammer and sickle were being unfurled. It was becoming the familiar pageant of an outraged public.

I didn't mind the outrage. It was the pageant I had problems with: that habit of wearing a logo like the latest fashion. The trouble was that they were shouting other people's words. It seemed to me to be prepackaged: the kind of indignation that was kept on a tight lead, that was targeted, pointed in a particular, predictable direction. It all felt phoney because I knew the fire at Bragantini's wasn't the usual white death. It wasn't the usual story of a negligent employer cutting corners with health and safety.

At the back of the crowd I saw an old mentor. Giacomo was one of the local left-wing politicians, the sort that was so sincere and straight that he had never had much of a career. He was an old-fashioned type. He was still wearing the same fat-rimmed brown glasses that he had had since the seventies.

As I walked up to him he recognised me. 'Casta!' He slapped me gently on the shoulder. 'What's with the limp?'

'Perks of the job.'

His face had got even softer since I had last seen him. His eyes almost closed as he smiled and his white eyebrows looked like they were growing towards the light.

'I didn't expect to see you here.'

'I'm working for Bragantini.'

His whole face twitched as he blinked. 'How do you mean?'

'He hired me a few days ago. His car had been torched. And now his factory's been burnt to the ground.'

'Along with a young man.'

'I don't think that's his fault.'

Giacomo looked at me with grit in his kind eyes. 'Casta,' he said, 'a young man was locked in his factory at night. He had no contract. You've got to see that Bragantini's responsible for his death.'

I tried to nod and shrug at the same time. 'Someone deliberately lit that fire.'

'Why isn't it public then?'

'It will be, eventually. But until then, they're putting the heat on Bragantini.'

'Why?'

'That's what I'm trying to work out. And in the meantime, demos like this', I jabbed my chin at the loud, earnest crowd all around us, 'are embarrassing. You're dancing to someone else's tune. You've got it all wrong.'

Giacomo looked at me and frowned. He seemed confused, unsure whether to feel sorry for me or the demonstrators.

'Come on, let's get a drink,' I urged.

He looked at the piazza: the day's last light was bouncing off the yellow plaster. People were passing round flasks of wine. This was where he belonged and he was reluctant to leave. But he looked at me and saw there might be something else to it. He eventually tapped a friend on the shoulder, put his fingers at a right angle to his palm, and bounced them to say he was off. Two or three people shouted 'Ma dove vai?' at his back as we walked towards the nearest bar. 'Ma dove vai, Giacomo?'

Once we were sat in the corner of a bar with a bottle between us I started complaining. 'I just,' I didn't know how to say it, 'I just don't understand what it is about this country. We're famous the world over for our scams. Even the most famous scam in the world is named after an Italian.'

'Ponzi?'

'Right.'

He rolled his head around his shoulders like he was considering the thing. 'It's because we're creative,' he said, smiling. 'We've just got more fantasy than everyone else. Whatever we turn our hand to, we can't help being inventive and creative.'

'Creativity isn't always a good thing,' I said.

He bounced his head from side to side like he wasn't sure. 'Depends what you're creating.' He looked at me. 'What have you been creating recently?'

'Huh,' I said, closing my eyes and thinking of the case. 'Un casino.'

'Meaning?'

I looked at him, and repeated it slowly. 'Un casino.'

'You want to tell me about it?'

I gave him a brief outline of what had happened. I told him that cars were being burnt on land that was being eyed by a construction company.

'Which one?'

'Which construction company? Masi.'

He smiled and nodded, like he might have guessed.

'Someone is tipping him off about what land is about to be redesignated before the piano regolatore is published. So Masi seems to be putting people up to buy the land on the cheap. Not Masi actually, but someone inside his organisation. The company can't buy the land itself because it's too well known, so they use a frontman to do the deal on his behalf. At least, that's what they did last year.'

'And you've spoken to the frontman?'

'He's dead. Killed last year in Milan.'

'Merda.' Giacomo looked at me. His kind face was suddenly stern, like he realised the gravity of the case.

'And now they seem to be targeting Bragantini's factory. Only this time the land they want isn't up for sale. Bragantini's a tough cookie and he doesn't like to be bullied. He's not selling, and so they're lighting a few more fires. A young boy got killed and suddenly everyone from your side of the fence is pointing the finger at Bragantini like it's all his fault, like he's some kind of murderer.'

'Well, he's not exactly without blame.'

I opened my fists, unfurling my fingers in his direction to say he was right. 'But it seems someone in the commission is tipping off Masi about urban planning long before it becomes public.'

He was moving his head rhythmically, like he was listening to music and keeping the beat. He was staring into the distance, trying to think it through. 'Have you looked into his operation, seen which way the money is flowing?'

'The only lead so far is an agency called Casa dei Sogni. Some woman called Marina Vanoli got the contract to sell the whole block. Plus she bought the best flat going.'

'Merda.'

'What?'

'Marina Vanoli?'

'Sure. I spoke to her today. Or yesterday. I can't remember any more. Why?'

He was shaking his head. 'Merda,' was all he said.

'What?'

'Vanoli is Luca D'Antoni's wife.'

'Who's he?'

'Luca D'Antoni?' he said, surprised I hadn't heard of him. 'He's the assessore all'urbanistica. He's the person on the city council who decides about urban planning. He's . . .' He couldn't finish his sentence. Indignation or disbelief seemed to rise in his throat and choke his words. I watched him shaking his head. He was smiling and frowning at the same time.

I stood up and paced around the bar trying to work out what might have been happening. Marina Vanoli's husband was the assessore all'urbanistica, so any decision on planning permission went through his hands. It seemed probable that he was tipping off Masi, or Moroni, about what land was ripe for the picking months before the redesignation was made official. Moroni sent someone in to soften up the owner and then snapped it up. Once the whole thing had gone through, Moroni put the lucrative business of selling the flats through the politician's wife's estate agency as a way to say thank you. And it was quite a sweetener. All Vanoli's husband had to do was give the nod to a constructor and his wife would make a few hundred thousand. No wonder he kept nodding, allowing millions of cubic metres of concrete to be poured onto the beloved territorio.

And that, I guessed, was why she sold mainly new-builds: most of her clients were large-scale constructors who were thanking her family for their support. It was all, as Spago had said, legitimate and open. There wasn't anything illegal going on. Some people might have said there was a conflict of interest but there's no such thing, not to an Italian politician. For them, there's only a coincidence of interest, a delightful alignment of interest, a fortuitous coming together of interest. There's no conflict to speak of.

I felt a surge of anger coursing through me. I went and sat down again and looked at Giacomo. 'D'Antoni's part of Italia Fiera, right?'

'How did you guess?'

'If you publicise this you could walk the next election.'

I watched him draw breath, like I was asking him something he wasn't prepared to do.

'I'll never be anything other than a stone in someone's shoe. I might stop them walking for a moment or two, but that's about it. I'll never walk an election.'

'But this would give you a huge advantage.'

He didn't say anything, just stared at me with those pensive eyes.

'What?' I said.

'Be very careful, Casta,' he said. 'If this is as big as you suggest, there'll be a lot more to it than you know. You go public with something like this, the players will be out of sight before the ink is dry. If you want justice, you sometimes have to be cautious. You have to wait for justice, be patient.'

'Yeah, just wait for it to come to you. There's a thin line between caution and collusion.'

'I know,' he said, taking off his glasses and holding the top of his nose. 'I've walked it all my life. Every politician does.'

'I've never understood that,' I spat, too aggressively. 'I mean, why doesn't an opposition oppose, like it does in every other country?'

He put his glasses back on and stared at me. 'I can only answer for myself. If I went public with everything I know about the ruling party,' he shook his head and laughed bitterly, 'I could cause a crisis, no doubt. But I don't, and I'll tell you why not. I've learnt that the more cynical the public is about politicians, the more they vote cynically. And that means the most cynical politicians get elected. It means there's no room for idealism any more. No one trusts you any more if you say you care about education or health-care or poverty. Look what's happening nationally. It's now so accepted that politicians are in it for themselves that anyone who says otherwise is less trusted than someone who admits it up front. I don't want to add to that cynicism. I don't want to give the public any more reason to think their politicians are all corrupt.'

'Even if they are?'

'Don't be ridiculous.' He smiled. 'Not all of them are. Not even the majority are. What are you really interested in?' he asked gently. 'The state of our democracy?' He did a slow-motion blink as he tilted the top of his head. 'I don't think so. Do you really care about corrupt politicians?' He stared at me through doubtful eyebrows. 'Hm?' He shook his head. 'You're only concerned about Tommy Mbora. You want justice for a young boy. For all I know, you think that if you get justice for him you get a slice for yourself. Hell, I know you're owed some.'

'This isn't about me.'

He looked through those distrusting eyebrows again. 'Of course it's about you. Everything we do is personal. Life was unfair to you. You lost both parents. There's nothing more unfair. So you're trying to make up for it. You race around trying to get justice for the little guy. Whoever he is, wherever he is.'

I shrugged. I didn't want to talk about me. 'Same as you,' I said.

'Sure, it's personal with me too.' He smiled. He said 'personal' like he was preparing for a fight. 'But if you want to get to the heart of it, you've got to play the game.'

'What game?'

'The game they're playing.'

'What are you talking about?'

'I'm saying you can't rush in and shout "thief".'

'Or murderer?'

He ignored me. 'All you would be doing is tipping off the big players, telling them all that they should run for cover. Believe me, if you want to build a case, you have to build it, you can't take the first brick you find and throw it to the crowd. That just draws attention to yourself and hurts the wrong people.'

I was shaking my head angrily. I felt like I was pumping the accelerator of a car in neutral. I was desperate to do something, but I felt impotent and here was the man I trusted more than any other telling me to stay like that. To go with the flow. He was almost double my age and half my speed and I suddenly felt there was a gulf between us. I felt the old furies rising up. I tried to douse them with a swig of the wine but, as always, that only gave them strength.

Giacomo could see what was happening and put a hand on my forearm. 'Casta,' he said gently, 'Casta, look at me.'

It took an effort to aim my stare in his direction.

'I hate what goes on here as much as you do,' he said. 'I've dedicated my life to trying to change the system, you know I have. But you can't just stand up and denounce the lot. You'd have every part of the establishment on your back. You'd have their usual attack dogs let off the lead and pointed in your direction. You don't even know what went on yet.'

I was almost dizzy with anger. Shaking my head in frustration, I felt him squeeze my arm. 'You've got an idea.' I heard his voice. 'You've got a circle of corruption. Politician to businessman and back to politician's family. I see it all the time. But you've got to get inside that circle. It's no good pointing at it and shouting for people to come and have a look. It's like pointing at a child's bubble: as soon as you touch it it disappears.'

'So what do I do?'

'You've got to assume they're more worried about losing a business opportunity than losing a twenty-two-year-old boy. They still want that land. They don't care whether it's got blood on it.'

I looked up at him. It was the first time he had suggested there was something positive that could be done. He patted my arm as if to emphasise the point. He was giving me the same advice I had given Bragantini: that he should pretend he wanted to sell. Only that way could we see who stepped forward.

'The carrot rather than the stick?'

He nodded, grimacing slightly as if it went against his instincts as much as mine. 'You have to deal with them to know who they are. You have to get close to them.'

I stared at the table, hearing his words as if they were coming from miles away. Most people who got sucked into the system started that way. Justifying their presence inside it by saying they just wanted to understand it. They wanted to

133

know how it worked, so they could know how to bring it down. Only most of them eventually got sucked in. They started doing deals themselves. They got too close and couldn't pull out the knife or slip off the cuffs any more.

I breathed deeply and recovered my composure.

'You OK?' he asked.

I nodded. 'Can you do me a favour?'

He nodded quickly like it was obvious.

'Tell me who's pushing the "Bragantini Assassino" slogan in your party. I want to know if someone your end is stirring up the campaign against him.'

'What do you mean?'

'It suits everyone to paint my client as the fall guy, as the evil padrone. It suits your side because your followers love nothing better than proof that the landowning classes are ruthless profiteers.'

He winced at my parody of his politics, but said nothing.

'And the ruling party will be happy because they want all the heat on him, not themselves. Someone in the giunta wants that land sold and they'll be happy to see Bragantini under as much pressure as possible.'

'And you think someone is puppeteering?'

'Someone's pulling the strings. Someone from Italia Fiera will be making your lot dance to their tune.'

'I hope you're wrong.'

'You'll let me know?'

He nodded wearily, staring into his glass before draining it. He put it down slowly and we looked at each other without saying anything. I left my wine unfinished and we headed out into the warm night air.

The demonstration was breaking up and Giacomo and I shook hands on the corner of the square. 'Mi raccomando,' he said, before walking off to join his comrades.

It was another beautiful spring evening. As I walked towards the river, I could just see the black outline of the Apennines in the distance. I leant over the balustrades and stared at the river, at all the water that had washed down from those mountains as the snow had melted. It glistened in the last light of the sun.

Everything looked stunning: there was just a trace of blue light left on the horizon and above it the sky went orange and black. I could see young couples walking towards the Parco Ducale, the dimming light adding intimacy to their stroll. I looked back at the Pilotta and saw its familiar bricks looking august and defiant. Bats were pirouetting above the line of mopeds that were making their way home.

Standing there, with the sound of the strong river beneath my feet, I could understand why people didn't want to hear about any more scandals. There are just so many already. We've all got scandal-fatigue in this country. It's got to the stage where it's repetitive and predictable. A politician suspected of this. A businessman suspected of that. It's only ever a suspicion anyway. There's no certainty in scandal, just supposition and guess-work and paranoia. It drives people insane after a while. There are people who have lost their bearings completely, who have lost the ability to be able to believe anything they're told. They end up driven mad by doubt and suspicion. It's so much easier to take everything at face value, to believe what they tell you. To go to the beach and swim in the sea. Go to the mountains and enjoy the slopes. Order tortelli and crack open the Sangiovese.

But then I thought about Tommy Mbora. Thought about his blackened body, lying there rigid and flakey like a half-charred log. That was reality. No amount of Arcadian langour could remove those images from my mind. I didn't want to live in a fairytale. Didn't want to swallow all that bull about the bel paese.

I walked home along the river feeling melancholic. I felt the need for company, the need to spend time with my bees. I wanted to be hypnotised by nature outside the city. I drove to the supermarket on the way to Mauro's house. I put twelve kilos of sugar in my basket and headed to the check-out.

'Sweet tooth?' smiled the woman at the counter as she fired a line of red light onto the barcodes.

I smiled and passed her a note but didn't say anything. I was too tired to explain what it was for. I headed out to Mauro's place in the country where I kept the hives and parked in the drive. The lights were on inside, but I didn't want to disturb him. I went into his garage and found an axe. I sharpened it on his stone. Within a few minutes I had enough logs and kindling. I took them out to the corner of his yard and lit a small fire. I went to get a pan and filled it half full of icy water from the outside tap. By the time I had done, the wood was hissing and spitting nicely. I put the water on and stood close to get warmer. I opened all the packets and poured them into the large pan.

As I stirred with a thick stick I could slowly feel the gritty sugar dissolving. The water was thickening into a mother-of-pearl syrup. I kept stirring, doing figures of eight with the spoon until I was almost hypnotised.

I always come back to the hives as a respite. Once you've

seen all the chaos and bloodshed of the city, you long for the busy serenity of tiny insects, each one performing a precise task for the colony. The bees seem, at first, to embody randomness, but the more you study them and watch them, the more you realise that every movement has a meaning. After a while that frenetic, throbbing hum of thousands of bodies appears beautifully ordered. Every dance communicates the distance and direction of nectar. Every determined bee is doing its duty, performing its allotted task for the benefit of queen and colony. I can understand why beekeeping has often been the task of monks, why the modern hive was designed by a priest: the hive is like a monastery where obedience and patience and sacrifice are rewarded. It's where the beekeeper can renew his sense of awe and wonder at the natural world.

But now even that is threatened. Disease and pollution and climate chaos are threatening the honey bee. My only form of relaxation is under threat, and no one knows the solution. All we know is that the problem is getting worse: there's less forage, less pollination, fewer flowers, less honey, dying bees. It's another, much deeper, dissolution of the monasteries. Suddenly, almost without warning, an entire way of life is under threat. The blissful, natural order of the world has been brushed aside and bees are dying and disappearing. The produce I used to get from a hive was about the weight of a sizeable child, enough to fill seventy or eighty jars. Now I'm lucky if I get two dozen jars. My only retreat from the relentless misery of the city has been taken away, and I don't even know why or how. It's as if nature itself is giving up on us.

I took the pans of syrup off the fire and put them on the floor to cool. I wandered up to Mauro's front door and knocked. A year ago he had been unhappily married and then unhappily divorced. For a while all he did was try and drown the memories and I was his preferred drinking partner. But then he met a hippie chick called Giovanna and she had done something to him. For the first time in years he had become sober and cheerful and fun.

He opened the door, looked at me, and grinned. 'It's the police,' he said over his shoulder.

'Who?' I heard Giovanna's voice.

'Coffee?' he asked.

'Yeah, thanks.' We wandered inside. 'Ciao Giovanna.'

He went over to the other side of the kitchen and put the water and coffee in the machine. 'Giovanna doesn't drink coffee,' he said over his shoulder, 'she only drinks strange teas. They all smell like fruit salad to me.'

'Lemon and ginger,' she said, smiling, 'or rosehip and honey.'

'See what I mean?'

'You should drink them one day,' she said. 'Might calm you down.'

'That's what sleep and exercise and sex are for.'

She rolled her eyes. 'I'll stick with lemon and ginger thanks.'

'You see,' he said to me. 'The passion's already gone after only a few months.' He looked over at her and smiled.

I liked Giovanna. She was some kind of alternative-medicine guru. She was gentle. She was taking propolis off my hands. It's one of those by-products of a hive which get in the way, but she said it was useful for her remedies. Mauro called her a witch-doctor. More witch than doctor, he said.

The coffee came to the boil and he poured it into two tiny cups. He put some water on the flame for Giovanna's tea.

'You didn't come all this way just to get a coffee?'

'I came round to feed the bees actually.'

'You already done them?'

'I've made up the syrup. I'm just waiting for it to cool.'

'Where did you heat it up?'

'Outside in the yard. I used a couple of logs. Hope you don't mind.'

He pulled a fake frown. 'They don't grow on trees you know.'

We laughed. I hadn't seen him this cheerful for years. Giovanna took her tea and left us alone.

I told Mauro, without specifics, about the case. I let off steam and, as always when letting off steam, my bitterness became apparent. I criticised the political class, the entrepreneurial class, every aspect of our local racket.

'The trouble with you', Mauro said, throwing his thumb backwards at me like he was hitch-hiking, 'is that you've got no pride in your country, no sense,' he was beating his fist on his heart now, 'no sense of what makes this country so great.'

I looked at him and raised my eyebrows. 'Bullshit.'

'Go on, then,' he said. 'What's good about this place?'

'You want me to prove I'm patriotic?' The challenge seemed stupid to me, but I didn't like losing a challenge however stupid. Mauro was hardly patriotic, but he had served his country, or someone's country, in various war zones: in Kosovo and Sicily and Afghanistan. He could point to his past and say he had served our weird and wonderful democracy. I thought he probably issued this challenge just to get one up on me, to show that I had never put my life on the line, which wasn't quite true. I was almost always in the firing line, it's just that I didn't have a uniform or an army to protect me. I didn't know much about history or wars or sport, the usual places patriotism comes from. I wasn't educated like Mauro. I tried to think of the last time I had been proud of my country.

'You know why eight millimetres is important in my world?' I asked him.

He looked at me and frowned. 'Something to do with firearms?'

'No. It's the measurement of the beespace. It's the distance bees always, in the wild, leave between one comb and the next.'

'So?'

'Who do you think discovered that?'

He shrugged.

'There are two kinds of people', I said, 'who have traditionally been pioneering beekeepers. Monks and Italians. The guy who discovered the beespace was both. Almost. He was a churchman called Lorenzo.'

He looked vaguely interested now.

'The guy revolutionised beekeeping. It meant we no longer had those conical wicker hives where we had to evict or kill the bees to get at their honey. We could now lift out the combs . . .'

'And steal their honey?' Mauro laughed. 'Sounds just like a priest.'

'He was American really,' I said. 'Called Langstroth. But

his first name was Lorenzo, so you can bet that his mother or grandmother was Italian. That's where the genius came from. He wrote a manual which is still used today.'

Mauro rolled his head like he was almost impressed.

'And you know who wrote the first, and still the best, poem about bees, having studied them using a concave mirror in the sixteenth century?' I waited for him to answer, and raised my eyebrows in sarcastic surprise at his ignorance. 'Giovanni Rucellai.

'And who first made detailed drawings of the anatomy of a bee and actually, along with a few others, coined the word "telescope"?'

He shrugged again.

'A guy called Cesi, Prince Federico Cesi. Know where he was from?'

He threw me a palm to say it was obvious.

'I-ta-lia,' I said, imitating the football chant by emphasising each syllable. 'And which are the most popular bees in the world? Which bees produce most new bees and honey? Which was the kind of bee that Lorenzo Langstroth bred, because it was so beautiful, almost blond, and docile? *Apis mellifera ligustica*, better known as the Italian bee.'

Mauro grunted.

'See, I'm proud that my little hobby has been improved and perfected by Italians. It makes me think we've got good eyes and brains, that we can improve the world for the better, and that makes me patriotic. You see, in my line . . .'

'Your line is crime,' he interrupted.

I shut my eyes. 'I wish it wasn't. If I'm jaundiced, that's the reason. All I ever see is the worst of this place.'

He nodded, like he knew what I was talking about. And, knowing what he had seen, he probably did. Mauro could be provocative but he could listen when he needed to.

'All these deaths just stay with you. I met a boy yesterday who was in the bloom of life and today all that was left of him were teeth and bones. You can't wash that thought away, you can't drown it with drink or sleep it off. It's there in your mind like an open wound, a memory that says life can be ended as simply as switching off a light. All you need to do is press a button, pull a trigger, and life is gone. One minute it's here, the next it's not. And that thought starts to paralyse you. Starts to make you think it's not worth doing anything. It's like trying to persuade yourself to start a game of chess even though the board will be overturned long before the end. If that's the case, it's hardly worth starting. You might as well not bother. You become paralysed by inertia and indolence. There doesn't seem to be any point getting out of the chair, let alone the house. I spend half my life sunk in that chair in the middle of the night, freezing cold but too tired to go and get a pair of socks. Those deaths live with me, haunt me. They seem so pointless.'

I looked up at Mauro. I hadn't expected to say so much, but it was just coming out.

'And the only thing', I went on, 'that gets me out of that chair at night is the thought that I might be the only person who can make those deaths less pointless. That the only way that any of those deaths has meaning is if I find out who's responsible, if I make it less of a random act and find out why it happened. If I can place it in the chain of cause and effect. It doesn't help those grieving for the stiff, but it helps me. It makes me hope that there's a reason, however wrong, for what happened.'

He closed his eyes and looked pained. 'I'm not sure that looking for a reason really helps.'

'How do you mean?'

'I spent ages looking for the reason my marriage fell apart. And when I found it, it was hard to take.' He looked at me with sadness. 'My marriage fell apart because I was always drunk.'

'I thought it was because you were always away.'

'That too. But I was sober when I was away, so I was drunk when I was home. You can't really blame Marta for finding someone else.'

'You can.'

He shrugged. 'I never thought it would happen again, that I would ever get together with another woman. But now I'm with Giovanna and I don't want to lose her just because I suck bottles like a new-born baby.'

'She's told you to cut it out?'

'Not at all. She wouldn't do that. She's not like that. If she were, I probably wouldn't listen, if you see what I mean. That was the problem with Marta. The more she nagged, the more I drank.'

'And boy could she nag.'

He looked and me and smiled at the solidarity. 'And I could drink. I'm not saying it was her fault, but you know.'

'I know,' I said.

We went outside and started feeding the syrup to the bees. Mauro lifted off the roofs, the zinc sheeting catching the moonlight as he did so. The feeder was a shallow, square bucket inside the hive with slots cut into one side so that the syrup could seep into a trough for the bees. I slopped a load into the feeder and then we put the hive back together. We worked along the line like that, taking off the roof, pouring in syrup, putting it back together. It always amazed me the quantities they could consume. Within a couple of days it would all be gone.

The local news was on the TV when I got back home. The fire at Bragantini's factory was the lead item.

'Yet another terrible white death has blighted our city,' the newscaster intoned. Politicians from all parties vied with each other to express their outrage. It was another case of a tragic death in the workplace. Bragantini, as employer, was directly responsible for a young man's death. The words 'manslaughter' and 'prosecution' were mentioned. There was footage from the evening's protest vigil in the piazza. The general public were interviewed and they, too, expressed disgust. The whole report managed to make it look black and white: Bragantini was a pantomime villain, the person the popolo should boo and hiss. He was the reason poor Tommy had died. No mention of arson, of construction contracts and corrupt politicians. The whole charade infuriated me. People's sincere indignation was being manipulated. They were being told that Bragantini was responsible for a young immigrant's death and being encouraged to give it to him with both barrels.

There was a brief report about Tommy Mbora. It said he was a recent immigrant from Cameroon. There was a photograph of him smiling in his Inter top. They were playing music over the report just in case the heartstrings weren't being tugged sufficiently hard. Poor Tommy, who had been anonymous in life, was becoming an icon in death. Another one of those names that stood for the injustice of the system, that would be repeated whenever someone wanted to make a political point about the padroni and the little people.

I switched it off and just sat in the chair. I don't know what time I got up and crawled into bed, but it was black, quiet and cold by then.

The first thing I did in the morning was to walk round to the offices of the city council and demand a meeting with the assessore all'urbanistica. The cool receptionist, a young man whose tie was knotted wider than his chin, said that the assessore was in meetings all day. He suggested I write a letter.

I drew my lips over my teeth to offer him a fake smile. 'Give him this,' I passed my usual business card, 'and tell him that I want to see him to talk about Giulio Moroni. Giulio Moroni,' I repeated.

The receptionist looked at the card and then back at me. He stood up and went through a glass door. He came back a few minutes later to say that someone would be with me shortly. I sat on one of the chairs and read a promotional publication about the province. There were the same people pictured in every photograph. The same local politicians in hard-hats and sashes, shaking hands with businessmen in suits. I put the magazine down and watched the councillors coming and going. It was strange seeing people who were at each other's throats in elections walking through the foyer patting each other on the back.

Anyone who has lived here for long enough has seen it all before: opposing sides of the political spectrum ferociously criticising each other, getting hot under the collar about this and that, bringing up all sorts of allegations and innuendos.

Then just as it looks as if the argument is about to get physical, harmony breaks out. A dialogue is opened, an accord or a compromise is found. And suddenly, just as quickly as it came, all that fiery rhetoric subsides and everyone realises it was all synthetic, put on for show when all along some deal was imminent anyway. It's as if every politician is merely an actor in a little theatre, and as soon as the curtain falls and the public can't see them any more they all slap each other on the back, tot up the takings and go out for an expensive meal.

After about half an hour a woman came into the reception. 'Castagnetti?'

I stood up.

'You're waiting to see Mr D'Antoni? Come this way please.'

She led me up some stone stairs to another waiting room. I sat there for another hour.

Eventually the wooden double doors swung open and a mini entourage emerged. The two security men were wearing black suits whose sleeves looked too thin for their thick arms. They were glancing left and right as if looking for trouble. They had transparent plastic tubes running from their ears into their collars as if they were in radio contact. The assessore had thin glasses on the end of his narrow nose. His white hair looked like it had been painted on. He had a narrow, formal face but his eyelids covered up half his pupils as if he were bored by life or had something to hide. It was easy to recognise him from the huge posters that were slapped up all over the place at every election. Like everything in this country, even an election was a beauty contest.

'You're this Castagnetti?' he said, like it was an accusation.

I nodded.

'Let's talk outside. I've been in meetings all morning. I need some fresh air.'

We walked out of the waiting room and onto the corridor outside. It was a stone balcony which ran around the interior of the palazzo. I watched his heavies fan out to a discreet distance. They put their knuckles on the stone balcony to lean over the edge. They were scanning the whole area like someone might take a pot-shot at this local cowboy any minute. They looked ridiculous, but they made the assessore look important and that, more than protection, was their purpose.

'So you're a private investigator?'

'That's right.'

'Did the opposition hire you?' he said drily, a hint of a smile on his lips. It was a smile that reminded me of a knife in moonlight.

'No. Bragantini did.'

He frowned. 'Who's that?'

'Owns a factory on the outskirts of town. Burnt down the other night. A young boy was killed.'

His mouth lost its hint of humour. He shook his head slowly, staring at me through his lazy eyelids.

'You didn't hear about the fire that killed a young man, a boy called Tommy Mbora? There's been little else on the news for the last twenty-four hours.'

His face was a picture of controlled contempt. He didn't say anything.

'He was a young immigrant. Brought in to protect Bragantini's property from a series of arson attacks.' I said it slowly so he understood. 'He was twenty-two years old.'

He moved his face closer, so that I could smell the coffee on his breath. 'Your tone seems to be implying', he said icily, 'that I'm responsible for his death.'

'In this country no one's ever responsible are they? It's always someone else's fault.'

'It's not on my conscience.'

'Doesn't sound like you have a conscience to put it on.'

He stared at me from underneath those heavy eyelids. 'What is it you're after?' He said it like his job was to grant favours, which in a way it was.

'Someone's been lighting fires to intimidate Bragantini. They're trying to buy his land and using the usual thuggery: burning property, threatening the owner's family.'

'Why?'

'Because the land is about to be redesignated as residential. The arsonist knows as much because someone', I looked at the assessore, 'tipped him off. That's why the place was set alight, to try to get my client off his own land, to persuade him to part with something he has built up over his entire lifetime.'

His derisive smile froze on his face. He stared at me over the top of his glasses. He had hard, grey eyes. 'So who's guilty of this arson?'

'I don't know who is lighting the fires, but I know who has been buying the land.'

'Who?' He was staring at me intently now.

'Amedeo Masi. Or rather, Giulio Moroni. I hear he's a friend of yours.'

He took off his glasses and held them at arm's length,

looking at the sky through the lenses. He pulled a blue handkerchief from his pocket and polished the glass. 'Most of us', he gestured down at the courtyard below, 'spend most of our lives trying to earn enough money. Giusto?' I didn't say anything, so he repeated the word louder, like he insisted on my assent before going on. 'Giusto?'

I shrugged a non-committal assent.

'We spend our lives tearing around just trying to make ends meet. That's what life is like, right?' He put his glasses back on. 'When you become a politician you have the opposite problem. People are constantly trying to offer you things: donations, meals, watches, holidays, cars. You name it, it's thrown at us.'

'Tough life.'

He turned his grey eyes on me. 'If I so much as have my photograph taken with the wrong person it can ruin my career. If I'm next to someone in a restaurant who wants to shake my hand it would be discourteous not to. But say someone snaps a photograph and ten years later that person is arrested for something, you can be sure that photograph will come out. In this country there's so much smoke people wouldn't be able to see the fire, even if there was one. It's all innuendo and suspicion and paranoia.'

'What's any of that got to do with Giulio Moroni?'

'You said the man was a friend of mine. I'm trying to explain to you that I don't have friends.'

'None?'

'Not in the sense you were implying.' It felt as if he were building a wall around himself, trying to keep me at a distance. He was throwing words over the top like you throw steak to a guard dog you want to keep quiet. It was a tactical distraction, not conversation.

'How about your wife?'

He looked at me with a face that was suddenly menacing. 'What about my wife?' he whispered.

'I hear she's got quite a friendship going with Moroni.'

He stared at me. 'What is that supposed to mean?'

'I heard he's putting a lot of work her way. She's got a contract worth a few hundred thousand to sell his flats. A few hundred thousand just to walk clients around the place. He also sold her the cherry on the cake, the penthouse. Now I don't know what sort of discount he gave her, but it's not hard to find out. See, it sounds to me like Moroni is being really generous to your wife, and that's not something I associate with a hard-headed businessman. It kind of makes me think you might have some close friends after all.'

'My wife is good at her job.' He was smiling, faking pride for his spouse.

'She's good at her job . . .' I repeated with sarcasm.

'There's nothing illegal whatsoever in what you've described. My wife is an estate agent. She sells flats. Someone puts a contract her way and you barge in here and accuse me of corruption.'

'I'm accusing you of a lot more than that.'

'What are you talking about?' he whispered.

'The last person to have bought land on behalf of the Moroni operation was murdered last year outside his home in Milan. Is that legal as well?'

He looked at me as if he were aiming a gun. 'You're making some very explosive allegations.'

'They're explosive facts.'

'You want to be careful where they explode.' We were staring at each other now like boxers at a weigh-in.

'That sounds like a threat.'

He smiled insincerely. 'No threat. Just friendly advice.'

He caught the eye of one of his heavies and nodded his thin head towards me. The man immediately strode towards me.

'I'm not interested in how your family makes its money,' I said hastily. I put out a palm to stop the heavy who was reaching for my shoulder.

The man was about to take a swing but the assessore stopped him with an authoritative click of his tongue. 'Give us one minute.'

I stepped closer and stared at him over the top of his glasses. 'I'm not interested in corruption. Not today. All I want to know is who's lighting these fires. I know why. I just need a name.'

He laughed freely, as if he were genuinely amused. He looked up at me and shook his head. 'I didn't even know there had been any fires until three minutes ago, and now you expect me to tell you who's responsible.' He chuckled again.

There was something about his breezy amusement that irritated me. Two people had lost their lives because of this land-scam and one, my client, was about to lose his livelihood. And here was the man at the top of the tree sniggering away like it was all terribly funny.

'If I don't get a name,' I said, 'I'll go public with everything.' I leant as close as I could bear to his ear. 'It'll put your name in the gutter with two stiffs.'

'I'm afraid', he said almost bashfully, 'that I'm unable to help you.'

'Find out who's been lighting those fires.'

He shook his head, raising his shoulders at the same time as if it were impossible.

'You know Moroni, the gentleman who muscled his way into the Masi outfit? He's the sort of man who pays for everything in cash, if you know what I mean. He doesn't seem to listen to me. I figure he might listen to someone', I looked down at the diminutive politician, 'of your stature.'

'What makes you think he'll give up any information?'

'Because you'll tell him that if he doesn't co-operate he'll never win another contract in his life.'

'You overestimate the amount of power I have. People like him don't listen to men like me.'

'He will if you threaten to turn the taps off.'

He looked at me with incredulity. He didn't seem used to being cajoled into any course of action, least of all asking a gentleman to give up their muscle.

'It's your career on the line.' I put a card in the breast pocket of his suit.

His smouldering stare suggested it was my life on the line too. But then, I knew that anyway. When there's a link between a politician and a stiff, they do away with the link. That's the way it's always been.

'Anything happens to me', I whispered to him, 'and you can kiss goodbye to your reputation. I know who you are; don't let the rest of the world find out.'

I turned round and walked back down the stone steps.

Gaia, the girl from the petrol station, called to say she had found the face of the man who bought the cans of petrol on the CCTV footage. I told her I would come round. When I got there she was running the tape of the man backwards and forwards, trying to find the best frame. I stood behind her and watched the screen as a young but balding man walked towards the counter. He had a round, sad sort of face. He must have been in his late twenties, early thirties. He looked like he lacked confidence, like he couldn't meet anyone's eyes.

We watched him on the screen handing over cash. She fast-forwarded the images and the man came back in again, this time to pay for the petrol. Cash again. The images were grainy but clear enough. I chose the best frame and she printed it off and passed it over to me.

'Can you save that entire sequence?' I asked.

'I have already.' She passed me a disk.

I thanked her and walked back to my flat. I put the disk in the computer and watched him again. The camera must have been up high because most of the shot was of his pate and forehead, but his mug was fairly clear. I took out the print-off and wrote a quick sentence underneath it. 'Have you seen this man?' I left my name and number and ran off two hundred photocopies. I spent two hours walking round the city taping the mugshots to any lamp-post or wall where there was space.

Whilst I was out and about I decided, on a whim, to go and see poor Tommy's family, if he had any. I walked on the other side of the river to a small bar where the TV crews had interviewed people who knew him.

The place had multicoloured rugs covering the windows. I pushed my way into the dark interior. There was a small bar in the corner that was little more than a couple of trestles with a plywood board. Old sofas with bright orange covers were pushed against the walls. It all looked very tidy and clean. The room was empty but there was a stereo somewhere playing sunlit afro-jazz.

I pushed my way through another multicoloured rug behind the bar and saw a small kitchen. A thin black woman was washing up, singing to herself in the way people do when they don't think anyone is listening.

'Salve,' I said loudly.

She dropped whatever she was washing up. I heard something break in the sink.

'Sorry,' I said.

'What are you doing?'

'I'm looking for Tommy Mbora's family. I thought you might be able to help me.'

'Eric,' she shouted, trying to keep the nerves out of her voice. 'Eric!'

I heard a noise behind me and saw a man shuffling towards me in the darkness. He was wearing slippers. He had a sky-blue Lacoste shirt on, which made him look like he meant business. He had a book in his hand.

'I'm looking for Tommy Mbora's family,' I said again.

He looked at me. 'Why?'

'I'm nothing to do with immigration, nothing to do with the Carabinieri.' I held his stare. 'I just want to talk to them.' I reached into my pocket, pulled out a fifty and held it out to him.

He shook his head. 'Isn't it supposed to be thirty pieces of silver?' His Italian was perfect. Just a hint of a French accent.

I put the note back in my pocket.

'You think you can buy anything,' he said. 'And because we're poor you think we'll do anything once we've been bought.'

'I didn't mean to offend you.'

He closed his eyes as if trying to calm himself. 'What exactly is it you want?'

'I just want to talk to Tommy's family.'

'Why?'

'I'm investigating the fire that killed him. I thought they should know what really happened.'

He looked at me as if he were weighing me up with his eyes. 'I don't know his family,' he said eventually.

'Sure you do.'

'Go home,' he said with a condescending authority that surprised me.

I passed him my card. 'I didn't mean to offend you,' I said again. I watched him read the card. 'If you change your mind, please tell me how to contact them.'

He looked up at me and bounced his head. I wasn't sure if it was a nod or a reiteration of his 'go home' command.

I walked back out through the dark restaurant and into the

bright light of day. I felt relief, as if I were back on familiar soil. In there I was on someone else's ground, even in someone else's country. I felt I had been trespassing. Perhaps it was just white man's guilt. I had tried to buy betrayal. That's how it must have felt to Eric. If Tommy was an illegal, the chances were that all his family were too. He wouldn't put them at risk just because a stranger started waving notes around. I had tried to compromise, to corrupt. It was an old habit and no one, until recently, had ever complained about it. But that man's reaction had made me feel ashamed. Ashamed that perhaps I really did, subconsciously, think I could buy a human life. I walked to the end of the road and got back into my car. It was facing away from the restaurant, so I could watch its entrance in the mirror.

I sat there like that for a few minutes. I could see the bustle of Via D'Azeglio in front of me. All the shoppers and buses and cyclists seemed oblivious to the quiet sidestreets. Even the odd person who walked my way didn't seem to notice me sitting behind the glinting windscreen.

A few minutes later Eric came out. I saw him in the wing mirror. I waited for him to walk past the car before I got out and started to follow. I watched him turn left, walking away from the city centre. He was easy to keep track of; there weren't that many black men of his height walking with his sense of purpose.

At the roundabout he walked past the edicola and into the Parco Ducale. A few years ago they had tidied up the whole park to stop what normally happens in urban parks after dark: love-making, muggings, drug-taking, or just people sleeping rough for a night or two. They had thrown down glistening white gravel on the paths, dredged the lake, cut down hundreds of trees and radically pruned the ones they had left standing. It now looked more formal, less threatening but less exciting somehow. There were fewer hiding places, fewer intimate corners.

Eric walked across the park and out the other side. He was heading towards the railway. He followed the road that went parallel to the tracks for half a mile, right to the outer fringes of the city. He walked towards the arches of a bridge, pulling back heavy covers that had turned one of the archways into some sort of temporary shelter.

I followed him inside. The blankets propped up across the archway were damp, held in place by bits of wood leant against the bridge. Inside was a dirty dormitory. There were dark blankets heaped over mattresses. You couldn't tell until you looked closer whether there was someone sleeping there or not. Near where I was standing there was a brown foot sticking out. There were twenty-five beds or so in that space, just enough to roam between the mattresses, like a path in a vegetable patch. The place smelt of sweat, of rotting rubbish and unwashed clothes. Hollow faces stared at me like I was the cause of their misery.

Eric saw me immediately and strode up to me. 'What are you doing?' he hissed.

'I told you, looking for Tommy Mbora's family.'

'You followed me.'

I nodded. 'I want to talk to Tommy's Mbora's family,' I repeated.

'I am Mbora,' said a young boy. He was standing behind Eric in the dark. 'I am brother.'

I side-stepped Eric and looked at the young boy. He was barely a teenager: thin and hungry.

'You're the only family Tommy had here?' I asked. I don't know what I had expected: a father or mother maybe.

The boy nodded.

'You want a sandwich?' I put my fingertips together and bounced them towards my mouth. He nodded eagerly.

'I will come also,' said Eric formally.

'You following me?' I tried to make him smile, but he was stern still, like he didn't trust me or my motives. I could hardly blame him.

'OK,' I said, 'let's find a sandwich.'

I pushed the damp blanket aside. I walked gingerly across the waste land, trying to avoid aggravating my weak ankle on the abandoned bricks and poles, and various bits of other rubbish chucked from train windows. But the young boy danced across it all as if he did this journey every day.

'What's your name?' I asked him.

'François,' he said.

I heard Eric talking to the boy in a language that sounded like gurgling water. We walked on in silence until we came to a bar. It looked unappealing, but there were panini in the window and that was all we needed.

When we were sitting at a small table in the corner, Eric asked me what I wanted. I told him I was a private investigator looking into suspicious fires.

'Who hired you?'

'Bragantini.'

He pulled a face like he was chewing glass. 'That man . . .'

'I don't think he's responsible for Tommy's death.'

'Why not?'

'Bragantini has been the victim of arson attacks. The fire in which Tommy died was just the latest.'

Young François was looking from me to him like he was watching a tennis match. He was eating like he hadn't seen food for a week.

'It was deliberate?' Eric asked.

'The fire, yes, almost certainly. But I don't think anyone intended to hurt Tommy, least of all Bragantini. No one knew he was there.'

'That's the point of illegals. They're invisible.'

I nodded. It felt like he was thawing.

'What is it you want?' he asked.

I didn't want to say 'justice for Tommy', because that's what all the protesters were saying and people like Eric must have been fed up with blasé rhetoric.

'I want to find out what really happened to him. Who lit the fire.'

'I don't think we can help you with that,' he said.

The boy tugged at his arm and they spoke in quick, urgent sentences. They both looked at me.

'You're looking for work?' Eric asked.

I shook my head. 'I'm not looking for work, not asking for money. I'm just after Tommy's family's blessing.'

Eric translated for the boy, who looked at me again as if he didn't understand.

'Why?' the boy said, looking at me with suspicion, like kindness wasn't to be trusted. I knew how he felt and admired the suspicion.

'Because your brother is already an icon. People are

161

claiming him for political causes. That's what they do around here. They sign him up posthumously to their party, their crusade. They invoke his name as if he were a martyr.' I wasn't sure if he was following. 'I don't want to do that. I don't want to exploit his death. But I want to know why he died.'

'Why?' he said again. He was sharp, able to see that behind my self-righteousness there was guilt.

'Because', I looked up at him, 'I feel responsible. It's my fault it happened. I told Bragantini to sort out security, to get someone to watch the place.'

He stared at me, motionless.

'I had no idea it would be that dangerous,' I said. 'I just didn't think . . .' I trailed off.

We sat there in silence for a long time.

'Capisco' was all he said. Not with bitterness, just matter-of-factly, to say he understood.

The serenity of children always amazes me. The way they take things in their stride that would paralyse most adults. He had lost his only relative in a foreign country. He had no one left to protect him and he was here, with a stranger, saying 'I understand.'

We listened to the noise of the outside world: the sound of someone over-revving a car, someone shouting a joke across the street, a baby crying. I looked at the boy as he was staring out of the window. He reminded me of what I must have been like twenty years ago: alone in the world, completely by himself.

'Where are your parents?' I asked him.

He just smiled and shook his head.

I suddenly felt dizzy. He looked so young and vulnerable

and I could feel the furies rising up again. I got up to go to the bathroom quickly. I shut myself in the cubicle and recognised the stirrings of another panic attack. I stared at the white laminated door and tried to breathe calmly but I sounded like a cyclist in the mountains, panting hard. The floor seemed to be floating and I could barely feel my feet. I put my hand on either wall and tried to steady myself, but even then I was unwittingly rocking from side to side. It kept going like that for a few minutes until I slowly came back to normal, standing straight and breathing steadily. My shirt felt damp with sweat and I suddenly felt very cold. I walked out of the cubicle and saw François there.

'Ciao,' he said.

I looked at him. He had stuffed green paper towels into his pockets and had a fistful of toilet paper in his right hand. I smiled at him and walked over to the washbasin, looking at my flushed face in the mirror. I could see the boy behind me, watching what I was doing.

At the bar I bought a couple more sandwiches for François and we headed back to his hovel.

'I'll come back and tell you what I find out,' I said to him.

He either didn't understand or didn't really care. He smiled like I was a strange alien. He was kind of inscrutable and I wasn't sure if that was the culture gap or his character.

'Understand?' I asked.

'OK boss,' he said.

When he had walked away, Eric turned to me. 'Shall we walk side by side this time?'

It was his first hint of warmth or humour. 'Sure,' I said.

We walked a few hundred metres in silence.

'How do you know him?' I asked eventually.

'François?'

'And Tommy.'

'They're from the same part of the same country as me. We're a tight-knit community here. We all know each other.'

'And how do they survive living like that?'

'You just do. I did. That's where everyone starts. Most of them are working, they've got jobs. Most of them are saving money somehow.'

'And they're all illegal?'

'Some are, some aren't. It doesn't make any difference for getting a job. None of your fellow countrymen', he stopped walking and turned to look at me, 'wants to do certain jobs any more. Street-cleaner, janitor, porter. They don't want to look after the elderly or work in a factory. There's plenty of work.' He turned and started walking again. 'Your politicians talk about expelling illegals, and whenever there's a crime involving an immigrant, the pubic demands action. But nothing ever happens. And it can't happen. You can't lose your cleaners and carers and factory workers. Take them away and the whole building will collapse. The whole of European society is built upon cheap, immigrant workers.'

'The footballers aren't so cheap,' I said, trying to lighten the tone.

'You know, to most people in this country, black people offer only two kinds of service. If you're a black woman they assume you're selling your body, and if you're a black man, they assume you're selling drugs. That's just how it is. They think that's all we do. They think we're all from the ghettos and that our only way out is selling either one thing or the other. People who are nurses, or teachers, or doctors in their own countries – here they're taken for pimps and pushers.'

'And what will happen to François?'

He was still silent. We just kept walking, watching the cars on Viale Piacenza as we got closer to the centre. 'He'll be OK. He's smart.'

I thought about the paper towels in his pocket. 'How can I help him?'

He looked at me with a weary expression. 'Why?'

I didn't know what to say. I couldn't tell him I identified with a boy who had lost his family. I just shrugged.

He stopped walking and turned to face me. 'If you want to help him, find out who was responsible for his brother's death.' We shook hands formally, like there was a bond between us, and he headed back into his bar.

I pulled out my phone and called Bragantini. I needed to hear some of his defiance. He felt like one of the few allies I had. But when his voice came on he sounded weary and broken. It sounded like he had lost the will to fight.

He told me to be at the l'Oca d'Oro in half an hour. I had been there once before. It was a smart restaurant in the middle of the city: starched cream tablecloths, beautiful waitresses wearing maroon aprons that were longer than their skirts. It was spacious and relaxed, the kind of place that has only one small table per room.

I got there before him and gave his name to the woman by the door. She went and looked in her book and led me into a quiet, cool room. They had left some of the old beige bricks unplastered. It looked odd, these snakes of wall left bare just so that you could admire some masonry. I heard other people coming in, giving their names and being led to other rooms.

By the time Bragantini rolled up, I was half-way through a bottle and had reduced the basket of bread to a few crumbs. He sat down looking tired and defeated. The halo of white hair around his bald head was unbrushed and his eyes had dark rings around them. He didn't even say hello, just nodded at me and reached for the bottle. He raised his glass and threw it back.

'You OK?' I asked.

He closed his eyes and shook his head. 'They're trying to put everything on me.'

'How do you mean?'

'There was an inspection at the factory yesterday. What's left of it. They wanted to run checks on the employment records. They seemed more concerned about the fact that Tommy wasn't regularised than the fact that he's dead.'

'He was an illegal?'

'I didn't know,' he said defensively. 'I didn't ask. He was just someone to keep an eye on the place.' He looked at me as if expecting a reproach. 'There's hardly a company in the country that doesn't employ illegals. They're cheaper, more reliable.'

'Slaves normally are,' I said.

He bristled and raised his voice. 'They get the job done. To me they're human beings like any other. I don't care whether they're legal, illegal, whether they've got two wives or three balls. As long as they get the job done I'm happy.'

'Tommy didn't exactly get the job done.'

'No,' he said, staring at his glass. He took another gulp. 'But normally they do, that's the irony. Illegals work harder than any of the regulars. Work day and night if you want them to. Never make any trouble.'

That's why companies hire illegals, I thought to myself. Employers can pay them a pittance and treat them like dogs. They have no rights and the threat of turning them over to immigration is better than any whip or chain.

'Did they find other illegals on your books?'

'There aren't any books left,' he said bitterly. He leant

forward and rubbed his temples with the balls of his hands. 'Listen, I'm very grateful for what you've done.'

'I haven't done anything yet.' I had a bad feeling that he was about to cut me loose. 'I've only just started.'

'I'm grateful. You've put in a lot of work. I thank you for that.'

'But?'

'But any further investigation on your part would be a waste of your time and, if I may say so, a waste of my money.'

I looked at him. He was different: no longer the self-made man at war with the world. He seemed to be hiding behind the formality of his new-found pomposity. Someone must have got to him and struck a deal.

'As soon as you issue an invoice for your fee and expenses, your bill will be settled.'

I looked at him with disdain. 'That's it then?'

He stared at the table and nodded.

'A day or two ago you were imploring me to go after the mob that torched your car. And then to stop at nothing to find out who lit the match under Tommy's bed. And now you're telling me there's no point.' He was looking at the menu, pretending to be concentrating on something else. 'Who got to you?'

He was too embarrassed even to look me in the eyes. Until then I had assumed he was scared, that someone had been threatening his family again, or whispering in his ear about how dark and cold a prison cell could be. But he looked embarrassed. 'This case is closed,' he whispered.

'Not for me it's not.'

He looked up at that. 'You're no longer employed by me.'

'You're worried about your family?' I wanted to hear his excuses.

'It's not just that.' He was still whispering, looking over his shoulder as he spoke. 'I've lost my business, lost the factory I built up over decades. I've lost my reputation. And now I'm likely to lose my freedom as well.'

'I get it,' I said.

'No. No you don't. You don't know who these people are.'

'I'm beginning to get an idea.' I looked at him, sitting there eating his lower lip. 'You're going to be prosecuted for criminal negligence or something. They're going to pin a white death on you.'

'There's a chance they might not.'

'If what?'

He closed his eyes like he was ashamed to admit he was contemplating a cop-out.

'If you sell up? I didn't think that it was so easy to cut deals with justice.'

'They'll still go through with the preliminary investigations and all that. There will be interrogations and interviews, but it will get buried.'

'Who told you all this?'

He stared at the bottle like he hadn't heard. I asked him again.

'There's someone who's put in an offer.'

'Who?'

'I told you it's finished. I don't want you interfering any more.'

'Someone's offered to buy your place? Who? We agreed you would let me know if anyone approached you.'

He sighed heavily, like I had reminded him of some youthful idealism that now seemed pointless. 'I just', he juddered, 'have to sell. Otherwise, I'll be dragged through the courts for decades.'

I could hardly blame him. Most people fold when confronted with the Italian justice system. The thought of being taken through the courts and the cronache for years and years was horrifying. It might never end. Each time you tried to clear your name it would be out there again, the allegations and accusation reprinted and rehashed. Even just the thought of it had broken Bragantini's resolve.

'What makes you think that selling your place will help you avoid prosecution?'

He raised his shoulders slowly. 'They haven't got much of a case anyway. There's no evidence I even employed the boy,' he said, avoiding my stare. 'It's quite likely he was the one that actually lit the fire.'

I smashed my palm on the table. 'I don't care what deal you cut with who, but don't try and put that poor boy on it in your place. Pretend you didn't employ him if you must, but don't make out he was responsible for all this.'

'I'm just trying to see it from a prosecutor's point of view.'

'Try to see it from Tommy's point of view.'

'He doesn't have one any more,' he said quickly. He looked down at his hands. I could hear his nails clicking nervously one against the other like the sound of a radiator warming up.

'Just tell me who made you an offer. That's all I need to break this case wide open.'

'It wasn't even an offer. It was just an informal chat.'

'Who?'

He stared at me. A waitress came and stood at his elbow, but he raised an index finger without looking at her and she walked away.

'Allora?' I said. I felt like he was almost off-balance, ready to fall. I just needed to nudge him in the right place.

His head was hung low, his chin resting on his chest now. All I could see was the top of his head, but his voice was quiet and clear. 'Somebody came to see me the other day. Said they could help me.'

'Who?'

'He was called Bruno. Young man. You know, dressed smartly. Wore a suit like it was the first one he had ever bought. Left me a number and told me to think about it.'

'Give me the number.'

He sighed and didn't move. Eventually he pulled open his jacket and took a sheet of paper from the inside pocket. He let it drop on the table like he was chucking losing cards back to the dealer. I picked it up and saw the name 'Bruno Santagata' written next to a mobile number.

'I'll keep this,' I said. I took out my pen and notebook and wrote the name and number for him. I ripped it out and passed it over. I put the original in my pocket.

'Have you called him yet?'

'No.' He shook his head. 'And I don't want you interfering any more.'

'Don't you want to know what all this is about?'

'It seems fairly obvious. Someone wanted to buy my factory, so they started playing with matches. If that young man hadn't been killed I could have told them where to go, but I can't. I'm facing an interminable investigation. If I hadn't listened to you . . .'

'You didn't,' I interrupted. 'I told you to hire a security guard, not the latest person off the boat.'

He sighed heavily. The waitress came to our table again, standing at a distance as if she could feel the tension. 'Una tagliata,' he said to her. 'And another of these,' he lifted up the bottle by its neck.

She looked at me, but I told her I wasn't eating. I had all I needed from the encounter.

'Do you even know why they want to buy the factory?' I asked him.

He didn't reply but just stared at me sorrowfully. I thought I could at least tell him what was happening and why.

'There's another businessman in the city whose car was burnt a year or two back. Then the threatening phone calls, just like you. He decided to sell. And within a few months he discovered his factory was within the new development belt of the city and that the people he had sold to had doubled their investment. You know what the piano regolatore is?'

He nodded wearily.

'The new piano is going to be published this autumn. This Bruno, whoever he is, will be given a green light to develop your factory. And at that point he will probably sell to Masi Costruzioni and make a mint.'

He was still staring at me, his bottom lip protruding in disdain. 'I can't stay there, I just can't. They'll drag me through the courts for years.'

'And you think they won't just because you sell up?'

172

'That's what this Bruno said. He seemed sure it would all go quiet.'

'Sounds like I should have a chat with him. Buon appetito.' I stood up and walked out.

By the entrance to the restaurant I saw a woman at the door welcoming a couple into the establishment. She smiled, asked their names and went to find their booking in her wide diary. She walked them to their table and then came back to her station, smiling at me. 'Can I help?'

'Maybe,' I said slowly, still trying to work out what to do. 'I was expecting to see friends here,' I tried to look lost, 'and it doesn't look like they've turned up.'

'Let me check if they've got a booking.' She picked up her bible and brought it over to me. 'What was their name?'

'Ferrari,' I said, picking the most common.

She looked down the page, flicked it forwards and backwards. 'Nothing here.'

'Could I just . . . ?' I motioned to take the book from her. 'They sometimes book under his wife's name, they might have used . . .'

She passed it over to me. 'Prego.'

I saw the name Bragantini in capital letters, with a number next to it. A landline number judging by the familiar prefix.

'Nope,' I said, 'I must have the day wrong.'

'I'm sorry,' she said.

'Can I ask something I've always wondered about restaurants? When you take a booking, do you always take the person's phone number?'

'Always.'

'Why?'

'Just in case. It normally stops people failing to honour their booking if they know we've got their number.'

'And every restaurant does that?'

'Every place I've ever worked in, sure.'

I smiled at her. 'I'll just have one last look, if I may.' I gestured towards the tables. 'I might have missed them.'

'Prego,' she said.

I walked back to where Bragantini was sitting. 'Who booked the table?'

'Eh?' He turned round.

'Who booked the table?'

'Valentina. Why?'

'Your wife?'

'The housekeeper. Why?'

'Just an idea,' I said, walking away.

Outside the restaurant I phoned the number I had memorised.

A woman answered. 'Bragantini household,' she said.

'Valentina?'

'Sì.'

'My name's Castagnetti, I'm a private detective hired by Bragantini.'

'Yes,' she said more cautiously.

'You booked a table at the l'Oca d'Oro restaurant for this lunchtime, right?'

'I did.' She had the usual defensive formality of domestic staff.

'And you left this number, Bragantini's home number, with them?'

'I did.'

'I just need to know one thing. Which other restaurants have you booked for him in the last year?'

'Only the Oca and the Cucchiaio.' She paused. 'That's it really. He doesn't normally eat anywhere else.'

'And they always ask you to leave a number?'

'Yes.'

'And you always leave the house number?'

'I wouldn't want Dottor Bragantini to be disturbed at work for something social.'

'Rightly so.' I said. 'Thank you, signora.'

I looked at the piece of paper Bragantini had given me. I looked at the number and the unfamiliar name: Bruno Santagata. I took out my phone and dialled.

The person who answered had a young man's voice. I gave him the usual story: that I was a courier trying to deliver a package but couldn't read the address. I asked him to give me a location where I could deliver. He gave me a street and number, said it was near the hospital.

A few minutes later I was round there. I rang the buzzer and he eagerly buzzed me into the building as if I were Father Christmas. 'Fourth floor,' he said. I took the lift.

He was standing in front of his door as the lift doors pulled apart. He looked me over quickly. 'Where's the package?' he said.

'No package.'

He half smiled like it was a joke he didn't understand. He stood there waiting for me to deliver the punchline if not the parcel. He must have been mid-twenties and was dressed like a student: baggy trousers, a T-shirt with some slogan on it. He hadn't shaved for a week and it didn't look like his hair had seen shampoo this side of Christmas.

'You're Bruno, right?'

He nodded.

'Mind if I come in.' I brushed past him into his flat. It was

176

small and untidy. There was a computer console in front of a huge television. The curtains were drawn and the only light in the room was coming from some imaginary racing track on the screen. The air smelt thick, like the windows hadn't been opened for months.

'What are you doing?' His voice sounded weak and nervous behind me.

I turned round to face him. 'I hear you've made an offer to buy Bragantini's factory.'

He shrugged like it was nothing to do with him. 'What do you want?'

'Is that true?'

'What are you doing in my flat?' He sounded out of his depth already.

'I'm asking you a question. Are you putting an offer on Bragantini's place?'

'It's one of the investment opportunities I'm investigating.'

He sounded so full of himself I couldn't help laughing. 'Why would you want to buy a burnt-out factory?'

He stared at me as if he was weighing up whether to raise an alarm. But the opportunity of boasting to a stranger was too great and he took the chance to big himself up. 'It's an opportunity. I figured the owner would get a good insurance pay-out and might be ready to cash in the rest of his chips.'

'And how does someone like you', I looked around the room to underline my disdain, 'find the sort of money needed to buy those chips?'

'I've got investors on board.'

'Who?'

'None of your business.'

'Moroni?'

'Who's that?'

I repeated the name but he looked dumber than normal.

'Who gave you Bragantini's number?'

'One of my investors.'

'What are you intending to do with the land?'

'Make money.' He smiled at his little joke.

'Doing what exactly?'

'Renovating the place, rebuilding it.'

'Reselling it?'

'Possibly. It's an investment and investments are sold as well as bought.'

'Thanks,' I said with sarcasm.

'Land is the foundation of our portfolio,' he went on, not having heard the sarcasm. 'The yields might not be staggering, but they're solid and reliable. In this market, anything solid is worth building on.' His little lecture over, he looked at me with a patronising raise of the eyebrows, as if asking if I had understood. He seemed like a little schoolboy who had learnt all the right words, but didn't have an ounce of experience to back them up.

'And what gives you the power to call off a judicial investigation?'

He frowned again, like he didn't understand the question.

'You told Bragantini that if he sold to you he wouldn't have the Carabinieri and magistrates on his back.'

He laughed nervously. 'Listen,' he said, still talking down to me, 'when one is trying to buy a parcel of land, one is obliged to pull all sorts of rhetorical stunts. That was just one of mine. I wanted to make him think I had important backers, the kind of people who could wield that kind of power.'

'And do you?'

He wasn't the kind of person to talk himself down. He smiled like a cardinal with a secret. 'I know people.'

The poor boy didn't realise he was just a puppet. Masi or Moroni couldn't buy the place openly because it still had the stench of arson attached to it. It was still a crime scene and people like that stayed away from police cordons and Carabinieri. But they needed that deal and had sent in a boy to do a man's job. They had given him a cheque book and told him to go and talk to Bragantini, to soften him up, to whisper about how all the unpleasant investigations could be swept away if only he would sell up. And once the deal had gone through, they would take it off his hands, buy him out and start building some serious profits.

'You know what happened to the last person who acted as a frontman for Masi Costruzione?'

'I'm nobody's frontman.'

'Of course you are. You want to know what happened to the last person in your shoes?'

'Go on,' he said, rolling his eyes like he was indulging me.

I imitated a pistol with my fingers to make the point. He laughed like I had told another bad joke, but the smile froze on his face when he saw me staring at him.

'He was called Luciano Tosti.' I told him the outline of the story. 'I hope you're really good friends with your so-called investors, because they don't hesitate to drop bodies once they've served their purpose.'

He tried to laugh again, but his head recoiled backwards so

that he was looking at me inquisitively, testing if I was for real. I just nodded. He was still trying to laugh, shaking his head, but he was rattled all right.

'You're a puppet,' I said, pushing the point. 'And the thing about puppets is that the puppeteer can put them in a box whenever they want. The kind of box that gets put in the ground, you with me?'

'My uncle wouldn't let that happen.' He said it with a sneer, like his wasn't the sort of family that could be pushed around.

'Who's your uncle?' I asked quietly.

He muttered some threat under his breath about what his uncle would do to someone like me. He reminded me of one of those boys in the playground who responds to bullies by talking about how tough his father is. I suddenly felt sorry for him. I asked him to repeat it, but he didn't have the cojones.

He suddenly looked very young. He seemed to be uncertain about himself and looked down at his feet. I realised I was the bully.

'I didn't mean to offend you,' I said.

He looked at me briefly and then went back to staring at his shoes.

'You just don't seem like the normal sort of investor. Even burnt to the ground Bragantini's factory is worth hundreds of thousands. I'm trying to work out how you've got that sort of money.'

'There are people who believe in me,' he said, like buying real estate was nothing more than a question of people's esteem.

'You can't buy that sort of place just with belief.'

'No?' He looked at me and sneered.

I felt I had lost him. I had rubbed him up the wrong way and there wasn't much chance now of smoothing his feathers.

'Who's your uncle?' I asked again.

'You'll find out,' he said to himself.

'Is that a threat?'

He told me where to go.

'You tell your investors', I leant on the word so that the sarcasm squeezed out the sides, 'that Bragantini's ready to do business.'

He stared at me, unsure if he had rediscovered his dignity or not.

I let myself out, walking down the stairs thinking about my next step. I needed to find the boy's backers and find out the link between them and Moroni.

I went back to my flat and called Dall'Aglio. I gave him Bruno Santagata's name and asked if he had anything on him. And anything on his uncle. Dall'Aglio said he would look into it.

I was woken up by my phone. I tried to answer it but it kept ringing. I tried again, saying 'hello' repeatedly, but it kept ringing until I realised I was answering it in my dream. I sat up in the chair, found the phone, and pressed the answer button.

'Castagnetti?' It was a man's voice and he sounded angry, like he was blaming me for something.

'Sì.'

'What do you want?' He shot the question out like he was spitting on the pavement.

'Who is this?' I asked. I'd had my share of threatening phone calls in the past, but this one sounded more aggrieved than threatening.

'Why are you putting up pictures of me all over the city? Every time I walk past a lamppost it's like I'm looking in the mirror.'

'Must be hard,' I said.

'Is this some kind of joke?'

'No joke. A man's been killed and you're my only lead.'

'What are you talking about?'

I told him it would be better to meet face to face. He agreed with a tone that suggested he was going to bring along a grudge as well. We met in an ugly concrete piazza on the far outskirts of town. It was the kind of no-man's land that didn't feel like the city but didn't feel like the countryside either. There were vents on the floor of the piazza and through them I could see an underground car park.

It was late by now and there was no one around. I walked towards a dark corner, shaded by the awning of a shop, so that I could see him approach. I saw a short man walk down a staircase opposite and walk towards the centre of the piazza. He looked like an overweight bull-fighter waiting for the bull. He was pacing around looking agitated.

As I approached him I got a clearer view of his round face. He was chubby, with a large, high forehead and a large, low chin. He had an archipelago of moles across his neck and left cheek, like someone had flicked an ink pen at him. He looked like the man who had bought petrol from the Agip station.

'You're this Castagnetti?' he said, looking me up and down like he wasn't impressed. 'You better have a good reason for putting my face all over the city. Friends have been calling me all day asking what I've done wrong.'

'Good reason,' I said, motioning with my head to an opening in the corner of the piazza. We walked through it and into a children's play area. We sat on a rectangular, concrete bench facing the swings.

'Allora?' he said impatiently.

'What's your name?'

'Pace. Davide Pace.' He said it without hesitation, like he had nothing to hide.

'You live here?' I bounced my chin at a window at random.

'Sure. What's this all about?'

I was surprised he was so open with me. He had come forward by himself. He had already volunteered what I assumed was his real name and his real address. He had the wronged air of an innocent man.

'You bought two cans of petrol the other night.'

'Sure. So what?'

'Why did you need them?'

'A friend had run out of petrol. He was stranded out on Via Traversetolo at night. He had been trying to hitch a ride for an hour and had given up. So he called me and I did him a favour.'

'Who's the friend?'

He looked at me like he was suddenly doubting something. I wasn't sure if it was himself, his friend or me.

'Allora?' I pressed him.

'What's it got to do with you?' he stalled. 'I helped out a friend. What do you care?'

'I care what your friend did with the juice. Did you see him put it in the tank?'

He stared at the ground and shrugged. There seemed to be an opening and I tried to force it.

'That night there was an arson attack on a factory in that part of town. Petrol was poured everywhere and a young man died. All I need to do is talk to your friend to exclude him from my enquiries.'

He was still staring at the ground, chewing the inside of his cheek. I watched the moles change constellation as his jaw moved up and down.

'Let me take a guess. He's called Santagata, right?'

He suddenly looked at me like I had insulted his mother. His eyes slowly dropped to the ground and he nodded. 'How did you know?'

'That's my job.' I wasn't sure which Santagata it was, but assumed it was Bruno's uncle. The young nephew was front of house, making an offer to Bragantini, whilst his uncle was out the back pouring petrol through the broken window. 'How well do you know him?' I asked.

He put his chin in the air. 'We work next to each other at the market. Have stalls side by side so . . .We watch each other's stalls, you know, we keep an eye out for each other.'

'What does he sell?'

'Buckets, bins, that sort of thing.'

'And you?'

He looked at me with sad eyes, as if he were ashamed to admit what he did. 'Stationery. You know: paper, cards, wrapping paper. That kind of crap.'

'Been doing it long?'

He nodded, his eyes glazed over. 'Two or three years.'

'And that's how you met Santagata?'

'Sure. We're always doing each other favours. If I go off to lunch he looks after my stuff. I do the same for him. Have done for years. I know his business as well as I know my own.'

'Maybe not.'

'Antonio wouldn't be capable of what you're talking about. It's not possible.'

I ignored his defence of his colleague. 'What does he look like?'

'Antonio? Big man. He's got a beard, a chest like one of his bins.'

'Where does he live?'

'Boh,' he shrugged. 'Don't know.'

'I thought he was your friend.'

He turned round and looked at me. 'Sure. He's a friend. I just don't know where he lives. He's never been here,' he raised his chin to the back of the concrete piazza, 'and I've never been to his.'

'So where will I find him?'

He was slumped forward, his elbows resting on his thighs. He looked at me over his shoulder. 'It's market day tomorrow.'

'And his stall will be next to yours?'

He nodded, going back to staring at the floor. His anger seemed to have subsided, leaving in its wake confusion and doubt. His indignation and certainty had gone, and he looked worried.

'If it's true,' he was shaking his head as he said it, 'if it's true what you say, I didn't know anything about it. I just thought I was doing him a good turn. I've never been in trouble before. I never even ride the bus without a ticket.'

'If you're all that innocent,' I leant forward to try and catch his eye, 'you won't say anything to him about our conversation this evening.'

'What if he asks why my face is plastered all over the city?'

'Make up a story. Tell him someone was playing a joke. Or someone thought you had stolen some tissues from a tabaccheria. Tell him what you want.'

He was still shaking his head. He looked like the poor boy at school who couldn't get anything right. He had even got into trouble for trying to help someone out. I almost felt sorry for him.

'What time does the market open?'

'We're normally there by six. Set up by six thirty, seven, ready for the morning trade.'

'How's business?'

He looked round at me suspiciously, as if it were a trick question. Then he sat back, relieved to talk about something else. 'It's OK. This whole economic crisis helps us. People don't go to the posh shops for their stuff any more. They come to the market to save money. If anything, I'm earning more this year than last.'

'That's good,' I said.

He looked at me suspiciously again, surprised that anyone should take interest in his well-being. 'Yeah well,' he said, 'it's still not much. It's not hard for me to earn more than last year.'

Whilst we were on the subject of money, I nudged him back towards Santagata. 'Did Santagata pay you back for the juice?'

'He said he would give it to me tomorrow.'

'How much was it?'

'Can't remember. I've got the receipt at home.'

'You mind showing me?'

He cocked his head sideways, like he was growing tired of me. He half smiled as he sighed, turned the other way, then looked back at me. He stood up and beckoned me to follow him.

We walked back into the piazza and back up the stairs he had emerged from a few minutes before. It was a concrete spiral staircase, the treads topped by triangles of black rubber. He opened a door on the first floor and held the door open for me.

The flat was small and dark. It smelt of disinfectant and every surface was shiny and clean. In the front room there was a middle-aged woman slumped on the low sofa watching some quiz show on TV.

'My mother,' he said by way of introduction. We nodded at each other.

He told me to wait there whilst he went to get the scontrino. I watched him disappear down a corridor and then looked around the room. There were porcelain miniatures on every flat surface. It looked like the kind of room where a sneeze could prove costly. There were cheap oil paintings of the Alps on the walls.

'Make yourself comfortable,' the woman said.

I smiled and stayed where I was. I saw Pace walking back into the room holding two thin, small rectangles of white paper. 'Ecco,' he said, passing it to me.

I looked at them. They were from the same Agip station where Gaia worked. The time was right: just after eleven. The transaction for the first was 5 euros. That must have been for the empty cans. Then just over 11 for the juice.

'Mind if I keep these?'

'I was going to give them to Santagata in the morning.'

'I'll give them back to you in the morning myself. I'll pass by.'

He looked at me and shrugged. The boy did a lot of shrugging, like he let the world boss him about and the only resistance he could offer was to raise his shoulders. He walked me down to the piazza and asked me to take down the pictures of him. I said I would, though I wondered when I would find time. I asked him for Santagata's phone number and he took out a clunky-looking phone and flicked through it. He passed the phone to me and I wrote down the numbers. I told him I would see him tomorrow morning.

It was gone midnight by the time I got home. I photocopied the receipt from the petrol station and put the copy in my safe in the bottom drawer of my desk.

The next morning, the sun was shining and the place was full of people wearing sunglasses. For the first time in months people were sitting at the tables outside, shouting greetings to friends who walked by. I could see two women chatting outside the bakery eating rectangles of focaccia. It was as if the city had come back to life after its winter hibernation.

The shop door of one bar was wedged open, and the barman was standing there in his apron, talking so much into his phone that he barely had time to drag on his cigarette. There were cyclists zig-zagging between the ground-level cardboard counters of the immigrant retailers. An elegant woman carrying a dog in a check body-warmer was admiring her hair in the reflection of the Mandarina Duck shop, pushing her palm into the back of her bouffant.

I hadn't been to the market for months but it was just the same. The usual stalls selling the usual bargains. Triangular knickers were stretched on plastic rings. Hangers rattled under blue tarpaulin. There were carpets and bathmats wrapped in cellophane. A buck-toothed Chinese woman was selling faded duvet covers decorated with cartoon characters. There were buckets of shoes and dusty, plastic flowers with fake dew drops on the fraying petals. The whole area was filled with the amplified patter of a man selling magical cloths and mops. Black men were selling sunglasses from groundsheets. There was a wall of mannequin legs showing off tights and stockings. The prices were written on laminated sheets held onto plywood boards by crocodile clips. It was the kind of market where even the plastic bags looked cheap.

The customers were mostly the same types of people you saw on the buses: immigrants, pensioners, young parents, students. Those with no disposable income. Sleeping children were left in their pushchairs between the stalls as mothers raced through bins of loose clothes and fingered through CDs in thin, plastic slips.

I found Pace's stall selling stationery and picked up the nearest packet of pens. I held it up for him to see, he said 'three' and I passed him some coins held in the original receipts. He didn't say anything else, just nodded at me.

Next to him was a stall selling bins and buckets. The stall-holder was bear-like: a well-built man in his mid-forties with a beard. The skin on his face was loose, like it had given up the fight against gravity. He had none of the joviality of the other stall-holders. He looked like he was bored, about to fall asleep. But the eyes themselves were alive and alert, like coiled snakes waiting for the right moment. Before he had noticed me, I held up my phone as if searching for reception and took a couple of snaps of him. I turned round and took a couple of Davide Pace for good measure.

I walked up to Santagata's stall. 'Could I have a look at that one?' I pointed at a blue plastic bucket hanging from a hook.

He pointed at it to make sure he had understood right. I nodded.

He took it down. I watched his hairy fingers extend

themselves to lift it up off the hook. He changed his grip as he passed it to me and I guessed I had enough prints.

'How much?'

'Five,' he said whilst looking over his stall to check everything was in order.

I passed him a note and he nodded a goodbye.

'That your van?' I said, pointing at the white van behind him.

Another nod.

'I was thinking of getting one like that. Fiat, isn't it?'

As he nodded again, his eyelids falling even lower as if in contempt for a stupid question, I walked between the stalls to get a better look. When another customer took his attention, I pretended to be reading a message and took a snap of the number plate. I wandered off with the bucket, holding it by the semicircular handle.

I was feeling good. The sun was out and I thought I was close to breaking the case. Everything seemed to be making sense.

Sitting in the bar opposite the marketplace I watched Santagata closely. There was a regular stream of customers coming to buy buckets and bin-liners and the like. He never smiled. I watched him passing over goods and taking money without even seeming to speak to his customers.

An hour later I was uncomfortable and bored. The stool was too high, or too narrow, and I felt like an elephant perched on a pin. I had drunk three spremute and hoofed two brioches so I had icing sugar all down my front.

The bar was full of talk about some important game from last night. I listened to people's awe for the goals and derision for the linesmen. The brilliant spontaneity of the pitch had been replaced by the predictable paranoia and pomposity of the bar-fly commentators. Football's a way to reinforce that deep-rooted feeling that the world is against you. It's yet another reason to be indignant and that, here, is our favourite pastime. There's certainly enough to be indignant about. It's just that there are more serious things than a phantom offside or a disallowed goal that should arouse our powerless self-righteousness.

Then I saw Santagata walking towards the bar where I was sitting. He came in and shouted his order when he was barely through the door. He greeted a couple of people and took the tiny tazzina in his hand. I noticed how fat his fingers were as they held the petite handle of his cup. Close up, his face looked mean. Either his nose was too wide or his mouth was too narrow. He shouted for a glass of acqua which was immediately poured out for him and put on the counter. He slapped a couple of coins on the counter, the metal making a loud crack as he did so, and walked out without saying another word. I watched him walk back to his stall, nodding at Davide Pace to say he had returned.

I took a piece of paper out of my pocket and looked at the number. I dialled it and listened to it ring, watching Santagata reaching for his pocket. I placed my dictaphone next to my ear. It rang for five rings before a gruff voice came on the line. 'Pronto.'

'Salve,' I said, 'you left your number with my secretary. I'm just returning your call.'

'Who is this?'

I made up a name and a company.

'You must have the wrong number.' The voice was harsh and impatient.

'So who am I speaking to?'

There was a pause before he said goodbye and hung up. I stopped the dictaphone and listened again. The conversation was so short it was over in less than two seconds. I listened once more and then put the dictaphone in my pocket and called Bragantini.

I arranged to see him at his house. He let me in and I told him I had something I wanted him to listen to.

'What's that?' He sounded distracted, almost uninterested.

'I've got a recording of a voice you might recognise. It's just an idea.'

'I told you, it's over.'

'Just listen,' I said, putting the dictaphone on the table.

Our short conversation was played back. The man the other end only said a few words.

'Allora?' I asked. 'Could that be the man that called you, who threatened you after the first fire?'

'I don't know,' he said impatiently. 'It could be. I don't know. When they phoned me it lasted a few seconds, just like that.' He seemed defeated, like he had given up.

'Does it sound like him?' I asked again.

'I don't know.' He told me again to drop round my expenses. It was a way of reminding me that my commission was over, that the case, for him, was closed.

I showed him the photograph I had of Santagata. He shook his head curtly like he was warding off some street vendor.

I drove round to Lombardi's place. He was the only other person I knew who had received a threatening phone call. I hoped he would be more helpful than Bragantini.

As I walked in I saw him slicing some coppa for a customer, his left hand moving backwards and forwards like he was rowing. Slender slices fell away, and he caught the upper edge with a small clip and laid them out flat. It looked like something he had done all his life, something he could do without even watching his hands.

'Some culatello as well?' he asked as he folded up the edges of the aluminium foil over the coppa.

The customer agreed and Lombardi reached for the culatello under the transparent plastic bar. 'This is really optimum quality,' he said proudly as he placed it on the squat needles of the slicer. The machine began whirring and he started rowing again.

As he was slicing he looked up and saw me. 'Buongiorno,' he said.

I raised a hand and smiled at him.

Once the customer had left, he came round to the side of the bar. He made a gesture to say he would have shaken hands but that they weren't clean. I told him I had a recording of a voice he might be interested in. I put the dictaphone on the transparent counter and pressed play. I watched his face as he listened: he was grimacing in concentration.

'Is that the man that threatened you?'

He raised his eyebrows and his shoulders. 'I'm afraid I couldn't tell. It was a year ago and that', he pointed at the dictaphone, 'was so short.'

The photograph wasn't familiar to him either. I nodded, knowing I would have to go down a different route.

'Some prosciutto?' he asked jovially.

'Thank you.'

'Coppa, culatello, gambetto?'

I threw my fingers in the air and he took one at random.

He went through the usual routine, placing it on the slicer and starting his one-handed rowing.

'That's more than enough,' I said after a few seconds.

He kept going, ignoring me. 'Ecco,' he said eventually, passing me a thick A4-size folder of aluminium.

I passed him a twenty but he tutted. 'It's a present for your family.'

'That's very kind,' I said, not telling him that I didn't have any.

He shrugged like it was no big deal. 'I'm fortunate. Business is good. You know, everyone's talking incessantly about the economic crisis, but people round here will never give up eating prosciutto. They would rather go without shoes than without ham. I've got roughly the same job security as an undertaker.' He laughed gently at his own grim joke. 'Death and ham, they're the only certainties around here.'

'Who's your supplier?' I asked. I had always been amazed that for an area that eats so much ham, you never see any pigs in the fields.

'I am. That's the only way to make real money in this line. If I didn't raise my own pigs, I would be nothing more than a shopkeeper. I would just be selling someone else's product. This way, I'm responsible for it. I know it's the best quality because I've raised it with my own hands.' He held out his palms to me and shook them to underline the point.

That's what I like about this part of the world. It's so sophisticated but earthy at the same time. Even the fine flavours of a delicatessen are just an extension of a farm.

'Buon appetito,' he said, raising his right palm to his shoulder as I turned to walk out.

I sat in the car and called an old friend who was still with the force. He had a family to support, which meant that he would sometimes look things up for me in return for some financial gratitude.

'Marco?'

'Sì.'

'It's Casta.'

'Salve. How you doing?'

'Not bad. I've got a scent and I'm looking for the prey.'

'What's the scent exactly?'

'A number plate.'

'That it?'

I gave him the numbers from Santagata's Fiat and heard him repeating them under his breath. 'I'll call you back,' he said. 'It normally takes a while.'

I parked and wandered around the city aimlessly. Eventually I felt my phone vibrating and pulled it out. It was Marco.

'Got a pen?'

'Got a memory. Go on.'

'It's registered to a guy called Antonio Santagata.'

'That's what I thought.'

'So what do you need?'

'The address.'

'Via Volturno is what it says here.'
'Number?'
'53.'

The road to the Agip station where I had met Gaia was full of afternoon traffic. I sat in the car inching forwards and feeling frustrated at not having a positive ID on Santagata's voice and face. So far all I really had was someone buying petrol and passing it on to a friend. The friend didn't appear particularly friendly, but that was no crime.

I parked at the far end of the forecourt and walked towards the booth where she was serving customers. Most of them seemed to know her; they stood there talking and laughing with her as they paid for their petrol. I was surprised to find myself feeling excluded somehow as she offered each of them her happy, honest smile. I stood at the back of the queue and she didn't notice me until I was right in front of her.

'Salve,' she said, her smile more contained than it had been for other customers.

I had the photo of Pace ready and passed her the phone across the counter. She looked at it briefly then nodded.

'You found him then?' she said in a low voice.

'He came forward.'

'I guess that's that then.' She said it like she wanted to be contradicted.

'There is something else.' I looked over my shoulder and saw one other customer in the booth choosing some chocolate. He didn't seem to be listening. I leant closer towards her. 'I need to check something out and I kind of need company.'

'What do you mean?'

'I've got to go and scout out a restaurant. If I go on my own, I stand out. People are suspicious. If I go with a woman, well, it looks normal. They don't notice me.'

'You need me for cover?' She sounded almost offended.

'Il Cucchiaio tonight at eight?'

'OK,' she said. We stared at each other for a second longer than necessary and I walked out feeling mildly euphoric.

I drove home and called Il Cucchiaio. I wanted to check that it did what every other restaurant did: take a number with the booking. I walked over to my desk and looked in the phone book. It rang for a long time before a sleepy voice came on the line.

'Il Cucchiaio.'

'I was hoping to book a table for later tonight.'

'How many?'

'Two.'

'What time?'

'Eight.'

'Two for eight o'clock. Can I take a name and a number?'

'Renzo Rinaldi.' The name rolled off my tongue so easily it sounded real. 'Zero five two one. Fifty-eight, seventy-four, sixty-two. Is that right? Hang on, sorry, I've just moved house and don't always get it right. Could you just read that back to me?'

'Zero five two one. Fifty-eight, seventy-four, sixty-two.'

'That sounds right, thank you. See you later.' I hung up and stared at the phone. It was a long shot, but if Bragantini's housekeeper had been booking tables there, they must have had his number. And if they had his number, the chances were someone else had got hold of it.

It was a short walk to the offices of Casa dei Sogni. The agency was empty but for the girl on the front desk.

'Is the boss in?' I asked her.

'Marina? She's just gone out.'

'You know where?'

She pulled a large diary towards her and looked at the right-hand page. She tapped it with her finger. 'There's some reception at City Hall.'

'You know what time it starts?'

She looked at her watch. 'About now.'

I thanked her and she said 'prego' cheerfully like she was surprised by gratitude. I looked at her again, trying to weigh up how much she was a close ally of her employer.

'Do you ever come across a man called Giulio Moroni?' I asked.

She frowned, looking sideways to the end of her desk. 'I know the name.'

'How?'

'He calls occasionally for Marina.'

'You've never seen him in here?'

She shook her head slowly, like she was thinking about it.

I walked over to City Hall and up the august steps into the main building. I could hear the sound of an amplified voice as I approached the main hall. There was a wall of backs as I pushed open the door. On stage there were three or four local dignitaries, including Paolo D'Antoni. They were separated from the public by a thick, twisted red cord held up on metallic supports. The man next to D'Antoni was talking proudly about the beauty of the territorio and the projected growth of the city. His sentences were so long and rambling that they managed to disguise the fact that the growth would destroy the beauty.

I saw Giacomo leaning against one wall on the right and gently pushed my way through the crowd towards him.

'What's this all about?' I whispered.

He leant his head against the wall so that he could whisper in my right ear: 'The publication of the strategic review of urban planning.'

'What on earth's that?'

'It's the waffle before the business. Makes it look like they've got a philosophy to back up their plundering.' He looked at me wearily, just in case I was in any doubt as to what he thought about it.

I looked round the room. Giulio Moroni was standing against the wall opposite us, staring at me. I offered him a false smile and he looked away. Marina Vanoli was sitting in the middle of the seats, her neck still looking twice as old as her face.

It all felt a bit like a sermon at Mass. No one was really listening. In fact, quite a few were whispering openly amongst themselves. It was just something that had to be gone through, something to justify what came afterwards: the slicing up of the cake, the division of the spoils.

The man was still talking, droning on about what the city

had been like when he was a child. He described the honest poverty of his youth and quoted one or two local poets I had never heard of. He slipped into dialect occasionally to prove he was a man of the people. He had lost his audience long ago, but he wasn't going to lose the microphone.

It went on for over an hour. Each local dignitary having their say. Giacomo occasionally made a sarcastic comment to me when the idealism got too much.

Afterwards there was a small reception. Flutes of local wine served with minimalist canapés. There were lots of handshakes and back-slaps and cheek-kisses. I watched Paolo D'Antoni seek out Moroni and chat to him for a few minutes. They were standing close to each other, each looking over the other's shoulder and they spoke into each other's ear. As soon as they had finished, Moroni left.

I followed him outside and caught up with him.

'Enjoy it?' I said when he was half-way down the stairs.

He turned round slowly and snarled at me. 'Eh?'

I repeated my question.

'I never enjoy listening to politicians,' he said. 'They talk too much.'

'Don't they ever tell you anything interesting?'

He stopped walking and turned to look at me. 'What is it you want? I'm beginning to get tired of you.'

'I just wondered what your connection is to Paolo D'Antoni and Marina Vanoli.'

His eyelids looked heavy with contempt. 'There is no connection.'

'You've never put business each other's way?'

He tried to lift his heavy jowls into a derisive smile. It just made him look more intimidating. 'What's your problem? You haven't got enough work?'

'I'm doing OK.'

He sneered. 'You're doing OK?' He flashed his teeth briefly. 'So why are you following me around like you've got a crush on me?'

'Maybe I have.'

He gave a single exhalation that could have been a laugh or a grunt. 'Why don't you get a proper job?' He lowered his chin. 'Being a snoop is no career. You're not doing anything useful for anyone.'

A couple of people came down the steps. We had to move to the side of the staircase to let them pass. Once they were gone, he raised his eyebrows at me. 'We could do with someone like you in the company. Someone smart, tenacious.' He nodded. 'Very good wage. Four thousand clean each month. A chance to get involved in investments whenever you're ready.'

I chuckled. 'I wouldn't work for you if I had starving children to feed.'

His face dropped and his eyelids descended again. 'You think you're better than the rest of us, is that it?'

I shook my head and smiled slightly. 'Not at all. I just think the rest of us are better than you.'

He stared at me briefly, apparently stunned that someone had dared to insult him. 'You should be careful,' he whispered.

I watched him walk down the steps muttering to himself.

Gaia was standing under the arches. She was leaning with her back against one of the square columns, her coat hanging vertically down from her shoulders so that I could see her figure silhouetted in the evening light. I stopped walking for a second to look at her. She was stunning in an eccentric way. Her blond hair was glowing in the last of the sunlight and it was so chaotic it looked like she had cut it herself in the dark.

She saw me and bounced herself upright. We brushed cheeks and I could smell a hint of perfume.

'You hungry?' I asked, holding the door of the restaurant open.

'Always,' she said.

A man in a clean, front-of-house apron shouted 'Good evening' from behind a bar. The apron was yellow with a vertical black spoon on the side. He was tall and was cultivating a professorial look with his glasses perched theatrically on the very tip of his nose.

We nodded our greetings and walked towards the bar. It was a cavernous sort of place: bare, beige bricks forming curved alcoves full of dark red bottles.

'We booked for two. Rinaldi,' I said.

Gaia looked at me, frowning slightly at the use of a false name.

'Of course. Let me just go and check if it's ready. Can I get you a drink whilst you're waiting?'

'Malvasia please,' she said.

'Two.'

He bent down to open a fridge door. He ripped gold foil off the neck and turned the bottle in one hand so that the cork popped into the palm of the other. He filled two flutes and pushed them across the bar to us, his fingers on their bases. 'Prego.'

We watched him disappear under an archway.

'Salute,' Gaia said, holding up her glass.

'Salute.' We clinked glasses and took a swig.

'You're a good liar,' she said, looking at me seriously. 'I thought your name was Castagnetti.'

'White lies,' I said to myself. 'White lies. White death.' I stared at the candle on the bar, remembering the flames the other night at Bragantini's place. It was strange how the same thing could be so soothing or so destructive.

'Do me a favour.' I leant closer to her and whispered quickly. 'Go and stand by that archway and cough loudly if he comes back.'

She frowned slightly again but wandered off holding her glass.

I looked around quickly and went over to a sort of lectern by the end of the bar. I looked at the page where it was open and saw the name Rinaldi and the number. I flicked back to the beginning of the year. Every page had a dozen names and phone numbers. Next to each name was a circled number, presumably the number of diners. I looked up at Gaia who was watching me. She looked the other way and shook her head.

I kept flicking through the bookings looking for Bragantini. He said he had eaten here a couple of weeks ago, so I flicked back to the beginning of the month and went forwards. There, on a Wednesday evening, was his name and his number.

Gaia coughed. I put the book back to the right day and moved sideways back towards the bar. I heard Gaia waylaying the man in the apron as he approached. I picked up my glass and walked over.

'Let me show you your table,' the man said, walking towards the corner of an adjoining room. There were a few other people eating and talking and the room had that relaxing sound of soft voices and active cutlery. As we sat down, he pulled a lighter out of the pouch of his apron and lit a candle.

'I told you it would be romantic,' I said as he moved away.

She looked at me askew, to say she wasn't fooled. 'Why are we here?'

'I wanted to take you out to dinner.'

'What's the real reason? Something to do with your case, isn't it?'

I nodded.

'And you can't tell me about it?'

I shook my head. 'You already know more than most people.'

We picked up the menus. They had thick leather covers, but inside was just one handwritten sheet of paper. The handwriting was flamboyant and illegible.

'I can't read this,' she said.

'You can probably guess.' The food round here was

wonderful but, because of that, very predictable. No one ever seemed to get bored of the usual classics and each restaurant had identical menus, if not identical results. I tried to interpret the handwriting: 'Tortelli, cappelletti, stinco, punta di vitello, bolliti vari . . .'

We ordered and ate and chatted. She didn't drink much, but she became more open, telling me about how her father had remarried a few years ago and how she got on with the new woman and their new child.

'She's only four. I read her all these fairy tales and you realise after a while how many of them are similar. There's always something forbidden – a door you shouldn't open, a box you shouldn't unlock.'

'A fruit you shouldn't eat?'

'Exactly. Only they always do, and that sets off the story and its morality: the separation from innocence, the dangerous consequences of disobedience, the quest to return home. Either that, or there's something that is allowed from the outset but only with the promise of repossession, or payment, in the future. There are all these stories of kings being granted their wish, but only if something is given in return a year to the day in the future: their daughter, or wife, or kingdom, or whatever. So they enjoy their wish for a year, and forget about the promise that was extracted, and live blithely and happily. Only the reader knows what's coming: the troll, or fairy, or mysterious stranger will return and expect the promise to be honoured.'

She was smiling at me with bright, wide eyes, as if I were a child she was reading to. Then she became more serious. 'In a way, both types of story are fairly similar. They're about the price of our curiosity or our desires. They're about honesty and contracts and conditions.'

She shrugged like she had said enough and didn't want to bore me. I was watching her closely: the enthusiasm of her hands, the intensity of her eyes. There was something exhilarating about her. She had a combination of childlike simplicity and adult intelligence.

'You know my ambition?' she said.

'Go on.'

'I want to be a children's writer.' She was looking down at her hands like she had said something that might be embarrassing.

'Seriously?'

She looked up at me and smiled bashfully.

'You should do it then,' I said. 'Write a few stories.'

She shrugged, like she wasn't sure she would ever get round to it. I leant closer so no one else could hear. 'This case I'm working on is a bit similar to one of those stories. It's about someone who was given something if he promised to return it a few months later, only he got used to his new possession and didn't want to give it back.'

'And what happened?'

'Not a happy ending, I'm afraid. I met his widow a day or two ago and promised I would find out who was responsible.'

She looked at me with what I vainly hoped was admiration.

'Why does everyone call you Casta?' she asked.

'Because it's shorter than Castagnetti.'

'And what's your Christian name?'

I laughed. It wasn't that uncommon round these parts but it still amused people. 'Yuri,' I said.

She smiled. 'Your parents were Communists?'

I nodded wearily.

'We had two Yuris in our class at school,' she said.

'We had a few in school too. It's like being branded for life: you're the son of lefties. That's why I just introduce myself as Casta. It's less of a logo.'

'Digestif?' The owner looked more relaxed now that the restaurant was almost empty.

Gaia asked for a coffee. I didn't want another drink, but I wanted to get the man sitting down with us, preferably with a bottle in between.

'Have you got mirto?'

'Certainly.'

He came back with a purple bottle and poured a generous shot. He left the bottle on the table like it was ours for the evening.

'Will you join us?' I asked him.

He smiled graciously like he couldn't refuse a client's invitation. He pulled up a chair and twisted it as he picked it up, so that he sat with its back between his thighs.

'How was your dinner?' he asked.

'Buonissima, grazie.'

'What did you have?'

We spoke idly about food and recipes and about which was the authentic shape of cappelletti: serrated or smooth. I'm fond of food but I get bored talking about it. I poured the man a glass of his own mirto, topped myself up and interrupted.

'You're the proprietor, right?'

'Sure. Have been for thirty-two years.'

I nodded with a slow blink to show respect. 'What's your name?'

'Giulio Morandi.'

I nodded again and pushed him my card.

'What's this?' he said, picking it up. I watched his face drop. He looked from me to Gaia and back at me again. 'What's this about?'

'A client of mine is being threatened. He's been the victim of arson attacks, threats, that sort of thing.'

He brought his eyebrows down in disapproving sympathy. 'What's that got to do with me?'

I took out my snap of Davide Pace. 'You ever seen this lad?'

He looked at it for a second and then passed it back to me. He was shaking his head.

I found the photo of Santagata. I zoomed in on his face and passed him the snap. 'And this one? Seen him?'

'Sure.' He looked up at me and then back at the camera. He tapped the small screen lightly with his finger. 'He was in here a couple of weeks ago.'

'For a meal?'

'No. He came in saying friends of his had booked a table. I did the usual thing and let him wander around to find them. But they weren't here. We looked in the book and couldn't find them and that was that. He went out again.'

'When was this?'

'A couple of weeks ago.'

'Did he look through your bookings too?'

'Sure. He didn't know which of his friends had booked, so I showed him. He looked down the list, didn't see them, and that was that. Never saw him again. Never thought any more about it until now.'

'Could you remember what day it was?'

He jutted his chin out and looked up at the ceiling. 'No, not really. I suppose I might recognise the names from the book.' He looked at the table as if trying to work out whether he really would. 'Hang on.' He got up and went through to the bar and picked up the book. He laid it on the table and flicked back through the days, shaking his head at each one. 'Ecco,' he said eventually. 'This was the day, I remember these names.' He chuckled, shaking his head. 'It's not every day you have diners next to each other called "Lunghi" and "Corti".'

He passed the book over to me. It was the same page with Bragantini's name and home phone number. I must have smiled slightly because he asked me if any of it made sense.

'Plenty,' I said.

It made a whole lot of sense. Santagata must have been stalking Bragantini, watching him at home and at work. He must have followed him to this restaurant a week or two ago and realised it was the perfect opportunity to get his number. He came in, made up some story in order to have a look at the book, got the number and wandered off. Until now I only had some loose connections, but now it was beginning to stack up.

'You're absolutely sure?' I asked.

He nodded quickly. I thanked him and told him he might have to testify. He kept nodding like it was no big deal. I thanked him and passed him a couple of notes for the meal.

We wandered out into the cold evening air. I was feeling elated. Gaia put her hand in my arm and we wandered around the city. There were groups of people still window-shopping late at night, discussing the cut and colour of the clothing on display. It felt like I was on the verge of wrapping up the case: I had the connections, even though they were threadbare: a restaurateur had seen Santagata scamming Bragantini's number. He didn't know that's what was going on, but he had described the scene. Santagata had called Pace and asked for petrol. All I needed was the link between Santagata and Moroni and the whole thing would fall into place. The entire chain of events would become clear.

'Where are we going?' Gaia asked.

'Nowhere in particular. Just wandering.'

'Where do you live?'

I stopped to look at her. It was one of those innocent questions that had an array of implications. She was staring up at me like she expected me to pick her up and carry her there.

'I live in the smallest monolocale in the city.'

'There space for two of us?'

'We'll have to squeeze.'

We walked towards my apartment. It felt like there was a bond between us now. All I could think about was what we would do when we got there. It felt as if our leisurely stroll had turned into a sprint.

I opened the door to the apartment block and, out of habit, looked at the thin vertical strip of glass that was my personal postbox. There was something in there so I opened up, pulling out a small envelope. Nothing was written on the outside. The envelope wasn't flat but slightly bulging like those envelopes that contain a birthday card with a badge on them. I shook it from one corner and the small bulge moved easily inside the envelope like it wasn't attached to anything.

I ripped it open, knowing instinctively what I would find. The slug of metal looked innocent enough on its own. It was still and harmless. But the message was clear. The next bullet wouldn't come in an envelope. I could feel my heart beating, I could hear the pulse in my ears. I knew it was the kind of warning they only give once. There wouldn't be any more communication. I either dropped the case or they dropped me.

'What's the matter? You look like you've seen a ghost.' I heard her cheerful voice from what seemed like a hundred metres away.

I put the envelope back in my slot and turned around. I took her roughly by the arm and led her back out.

'What's going on?' she said.

I didn't even want to explain. I wanted her as far away from me as possible. I wanted her in another city, another country. I didn't want her soiled by the sleazy world I was mixed up in. I looked left and right as we walked back onto the road, checking to see if there were any parked cars with snooping drivers inside. Couldn't see anything unusual. I still had my hand on her upper arm as I marched her towards a taxi stand.

'Stay away from me,' I said.

'What are you talking about?'

'They're coming after me and I don't want you caught in the crossfire.'

'What was in that envelope?'

I turned away and hailed a taxi.

'But I want to stay with you,' she said, turning round to see the white cab pulling up beside her. I pulled her closer to kiss her and she brought a hand up to my face so fast I wasn't sure if it was a caress or a slap. She got into the cab without saying anything. I saw her staring ahead as it drove off.

Seeing her like that made me more livid than the stupid slug in the envelope. I strode back home in a hurry, took the envelope upstairs and paced around my tiny flat. Before, I had been excited to be within touching distance of them, but now it just seemed that they were within firing range of me. I went over to the window and looked through the gaps between the tapparelle. I couldn't sense anything out of the ordinary.

I had so far avoided involving the authorities because the case was political and that meant that it wouldn't be played straight. There would be pressures from all sorts of unexpected quarters and honest officers would find themselves making compromises. Handing over my case to them would be like launching a paper aeroplane in a gale: it would certainly go somewhere, but there was no telling how or why. I wanted to hold on to it myself. At least until I had the kind of case that could only go in one direction.

But that bullet in the envelope had changed my mind. I decided to call Dall'Aglio, an old-style, abrasive Carabiniere. It was gone midnight but I called him anyway.

'Dall'Aglio? Castagnetti.'

He grunted. We were never sure if we were allies or rivals in the fight against crime. Sometimes I didn't know if he was even fighting the fight or just watching it and taking notes. And he had a grudge against me because I fought as much against the authorities as I did against the criminals. But we went way back and held the animosity in check for the sake of civility.

'I've got a very sensitive case,' I said slowly.

'And you're a sensitive guy.'

'Right.' I paused. 'This one's political.'

I heard him sucking air through his teeth. 'We don't do politics here.'

'What's that mean? You let them do whatever they want?' Before I could stop myself our old arguments were boiling to the surface.

'It means', he said wearily, 'that almost anything political gets referred to the Guardia di Finanza. Ninety-nine per cent of political crime is financial. I assume this one is too?'

'Started out financial. Finished with murder.'

The line went quiet. I could hear his slow breathing, nothing else. 'What are you talking about?'

'You know Pino Bragantini?'

'I know he's about the most unpopular person in the city right now.'

'Well, he shouldn't be. That fire wasn't his fault.'

I had known Dall'Aglio long enough to trust him with every little detail. As I went through it, I heard him sucking his teeth. He swore eloquently when I told him about the evening's little delivery. He seemed more angry that I had held out on him than about what had been going on.

'It sounds like you should lie low for a while, let me take this up,' he said.

'That's not my style.'

'No.' He said it regretfully. 'That's not your style.'

'I'm going to write a memorandum and leave it with a friend. If anything happens to me, he'll have all the details and the evidence.'

'The evidence should be here.'

'It will be. This time tomorrow you'll have everything. All neatly bagged up and labelled.'

'I just hope you're not that way yourself.'

It was as close as he would ever get to human warmth and I thanked him. He told me he was on night duty and to come and see him if anything came up.

I shuffled over to my desk to write a formal document about the case. I went over it in my head. Bragantini had hired me because his car had been torched. It had started out as a no-hope investigation into mindless vandalism. Cars get burnt all the time. It's the way city folk enjoy a camp fire. But then it had become obvious that the vandalism wasn't mindless at all but a well-orchestrated plan. Elements within Masi's construction company had been burning the property of people who owned land that was about to be requalified as residential. They literally turned up the heat. It had happened last year to Lombardi and this year it was Bragantini's turn. It seemed likely that they were getting their information from the assessore himself, because his unimpressive wife was receiving large contracts. Everyone seemed to be doing nicely but it was a costly game. Last year the go-between, Luciano Tosti, had been killed. This year a young boy hired as an extra pair of eyes had been killed.

It seemed very likely that Santagata had started the fire that killed Tommy Mbora. Gaia had seen Davide Pace buying petrol, and he had told me in person that he had given it to

Santagata. And the restaurateur gave me a positive ID on him, saying he had visited his place the day Bragantini was dining there. It wasn't watertight, but it was looking like it might not have too many leaks. All I needed was a connection between Santagata and Moroni.

I started writing it up formally. I listed the evidence and the various eyewitnesses: Gaia, the restaurateur, Davide Pace. I signed the report and put it in an envelope along with the other envelope I had opened an hour ago.

Mauro's place was all dark when I drove up. I looked at the clock on the dashboard and realised it was gone two now. The doorbell sounded unexpectedly loud. I rang it again and again until I saw a light going on.

Mauro opened the door and we shuffled into the kitchen. He was used to these kinds of visits and put the coffee on without saying anything. I passed him my envelope with all the details of the case.

'What's this?' he asked.

'If anything happens to me, give it to Dall'Aglio in the Questura.'

'What's going to happen to you?'

I told him about my little delivery. That woke him up. He whispered a few of his finest expletives as he poured out the coffee.

'What are you going to do?'

'Same as before. I'll just look in my rear-view mirror more often.'

He smiled, shaking his head.

'The worst thing about it was I was on the verge of persuading a young woman to visit my flat.'

He looked at me and blinked in slow motion. 'Who?'

'A girl. Her name's in there.' I pointed at my envelope. 'Anything happens to me, make sure she's OK.'

He nodded, staring at me like he wanted to know more but didn't want to pry.

'She's called Gaia,' I said.

We sat there in silence as we drank the coffee. I heard Giovanna going to the bathroom upstairs.

'Sorry to have woken you up,' I said.

'I'm glad you did. I'm coming with you.'

'There's no need.'

'There's every need. Just let me go and get dressed.' He stood up before I could even contradict him. He walked upstairs.

We had never worked a case together, though we had often spoken about it. I didn't really like the idea. Didn't like the thought that maybe I did need an extra pair of eyes, or barrels, watching my back.

He came down the stairs dressed in a flak jacket. He was carrying a long black bag.

'What's that?' I said, nodding at the bag.

'Back-up.' He zipped it open and showed me enough firearms to overthrow a small country. There were a couple of rifles, two pistols and various long objects wrapped in rags.

'That's not the kind of back-up I need, Mauro.'

'Sure it is. Fight fire with fire. That's the only way. Talk to them in their own language.'

'That's not the way I work,' I said firmly.

He looked at me like he didn't understand. 'Sure it is.'

I shook my head. 'If you really want to help me out, keep

an eye on Gaia. She never meant to get mixed up in this, and I want to make sure she doesn't get hurt.'

He stared at me as if he were struggling to disguise his disappointment. I told him where she lived and worked. He nodded, accepting defeat. I wrote down the addresses just in case he couldn't remember. As I gave it to him, I reminded him to put my memorandum somewhere safe.

'Take care,' he said as I was going out the door.

I found Santagata's address easily enough. It was in a nondescript part of town. I walked around the block to get a sense of where I was: there was a park on one side and apartment blocks on the others. I passed a large, rectangular skip saying 'urban waste' about fifty metres beyond the entrance to Santagata's block. Next to it were circular ones for glass and plastic with rubber triangles over their openings looking like slices of rubber pizza. I tried to look inside but couldn't see anything. I took out my phone, held it in my right hand and put my arm inside to snap a picture. I looked at it: a dark array of plastic water bottles but nothing else.

I stepped on the long pedal to open the big skip and peered inside. It was almost full. I looked all over but couldn't see what I was after. There was nothing for it but to jump in. I sank up to my knees as I landed inside, ripping black bin-liners as I did so. As I tried to move bulging bin-liners out of my way, my fingers ripped through the thin plastic and my hands sunk into household waste. I tried not to think about it. I had to throw stuff onto the pavement to get closer to the bottom of the skip.

After I had thrown four or five heavy black bags over my shoulder I saw, in the space between two others, a flat side of something green. I moved the bags apart and saw what I had been looking for: two dark green, plastic petrol cans. The

223

barcode was still visible on them. I picked them up by their sides, in case there were still prints on the handles. I let them drop to the pavement and then crawled out of the skip. A couple of late-night passers-by looked at me as I did so, so I yawned and stretched to pretend I had just woken up.

'Good morning,' I said to them, and they hurried away.

I put the bags back in the skip and put the two petrol cans in a metal box in my boot. Between them they took up almost the entire space. I locked the box and looked at my trousers. There were damp patches that smelt like sour milk and rotting potatoes.

The roads were deserted and I was at the Questura within a couple of minutes. Dall'Aglio looked me up and down and frowned. I told him I had been paddling in a skip and he nodded, like it didn't surprise him. I told him what I had found. I hadn't expected congratulations or gratitude, but I did expect him to say something positive. He was merely shaking his head, looking at what he had written.

'It doesn't add up to much,' he said. 'A couple of receipts, a couple of eyewitnesses and petrol cans in a skip. It's hardly the basis for a murder conviction.'

'Dust the cans for prints,' I said impatiently. 'If they're Santagata's, then you've got enough to bring him in.'

He shrugged, closing his eyes like he was politely trying to shut out the sound of my insistence. 'Unless you've got anything else, I don't think we'll be bringing him in.' He said it with a strange sort of conclusiveness, looking at me through his raised eyebrows to check I had understood. He leant forward and pushed himself up from his desk. He held out his hand.

I hesitated before taking it. 'What else do you need? Clearance from above?'

'They don't like surprises,' he said cryptically. 'If this case is, as you say, political, I need to understand it before wading in in the middle of the night.'

We shook hands, looking at each other as if we were squaring up for one of our fights.

It was still dark and the roads were almost empty. I got onto the motorway and flew past towns with familiar, flowery names: Fidenza, Fiorenzuola, Piacenza, Casalpusterlengo. The flat countryside looked all the same from the motorway: there were long, low warehouses and crumbling villas illuminated by the headlights of long-distance lorries.

I stopped in a bar on the outskirts of Milan. I hadn't slept all night and needed a shot of coffee. There was a blast of warm air as I walked into a narrow bar. It was full of people dressed for work. The barman had a never-ending supply of tidy, formulaic politeness – 'a lei', 'tante cose', 'di nuovo' – as he put people's change in the concave plate on the counter. 'Buondì,' he would say cheerfully as the door opened to let another customer in.

The handle of the tazzina was so small that the tips of my thumb and forefinger only just touched through the hole. The coffee was bitter, bitter but buono. I felt my arms coming alive again, like they were ready for a fight at last.

I asked for the local business directory and found the address of Gruppo Sicurezza insurance. I threw back the last of the coffee and got back in the car.

For one of the country's insurance giants, the Gruppo Sicurezza building was surprisingly small, tucked away down a sidestreet away from the noise. I asked for the legal department at the front desk and was sent up to the fourth floor. I watched an air-bubble wobble up inside the water cooler as I took a plastic glass of water. People came in and out without noticing me for almost half an hour.

Eventually a young, overweight man with hair like a soggy salad came out and introduced himself. We went into his office, a cramped little space he shared with a young woman.

'Prego,' he said, indicating a chair. He was sweating from the effort of the walk to the front desk. 'How can I help?'

'I'm a private investigator.'

'Investigating what?'

'A case of arson.'

'Aha,' he said, as if he had understood already.

'The owner told me he was insured with you.'

The man looked at me sideways. 'Right,' he said, drawing out the word so that it lasted a couple of seconds.

'He's the victim in this,' I clarified. 'Along with a few others.' So many arson cases are perpetrated by the owners that he must have expected it to be another case of the policy holder striking a match.

'So why are you here?'

'Where I come from quite a lot of people would like to prove this fire was just an accident. No arson at all. It's a politically sensitive case it seems, and that means everyone's happy for it to pass as a tragic accident. As always, that means you're the one who will foot the bill.'

He was nodding slowly. 'What's your interest?'

'Justice.'

He chuckled, thinking I had made a joke. Then saw me just staring at him. 'Really?'

'A young man died in the fire. You might have heard about it.'

He was serious now all right. Staring at me and nodding slowly.

'And how can we help you?'

'I want to get to the bottom of this case, but someone's taken my spade away. My client – your policy holder – has terminated my contract just as it was about to get interesting.' He was still studying me, trying to work out where I was going. I came to the point. 'The local authorities are under pressure to ignore the case. My former client looks likely to cut a deal with the people who destroyed his factory.'

'I don't get it. You're asking us to employ you?'

'Not only that. I need someone on my side. I got a warning in last night's post, the kind of warning that only comes once.' I looked up at him to check he was following. 'I need some heavyweights on my side.'

'Yeah, well,' he said patting his paunch, 'you've come to the right man.'

'I was thinking more of the company.'

'The company's pretty lean right now.'

He was a strange one. He had let himself go, but wouldn't let anyone else get away with anything.

'Do you want to give me the name?'

'Bragantini.'

He rolled his head in my direction. 'That rings a bell. Let's see.' He pulled himself up in his seat and waggled his mouse left and right to wake up the computer. 'Come on,' he said impatiently. 'These computers are like women. Sensitive and complicated and expensive. But they're getting cheaper by the day, and less reliable. They break down just when you're least expecting it.'

The girl at the other desk looked up and I saw her rolling her eyes. 'And most users are typical men,' she said under her breath. 'Always looking for an upgrade.'

'Here we are.' He ignored her. 'Bragantini. I've got a log of a claim going through yesterday.' He whistled. 'Big claim by the looks of it.'

'I can save you the lot. I just need a small retainer.'

He chuckled. 'You're quite a hustler aren't you?'

'Isn't everyone?'

He picked up the phone and asked for someone called Cavalieri. I listened to him explaining what was going on. We duly got summoned into Cavalieri's office. I knew him from way back, when I used to do freelance work for him at another insurance company.

'Casta,' said Cavalieri with open arms as we walked in. 'How did I know this would have something to do with you?' He slapped his hand into mine.

The fat man looked at the both of us. He looked a bit crestfallen that he didn't have to do the introductions.

'Prego, prego,' Cavalieri pointed at two tan armchairs in front of his desk. 'What's this all about?'

I gave him a brief summary, skipping the sensitive details. He took notes and tutted. When I had finished, he asked the obvious question.

'You're sure Bragantini's not involved?'

I raised my shoulders. 'Seems very unlikely to me. He hired me before the fire. He hired the security guard, of sorts. He wanted to get to the bottom of it all.'

'Only now he doesn't.'

'He's under pressure. He's facing bankruptcy and criminal charges. It's hardly surprising the guy's folding.'

Cavalieri looked down at his desk and then at me. 'He's no longer your client, you say?'

'Afraid not.'

'Then if we employ you, he's a suspect the same as all the rest, clear?'

'Crystal.'

He looked briefly at the fat man, who nodded slightly. They agreed to give me a small daily retainer. I expressed gratitude, but more for the unspoken support. I still felt exposed, but at least I wasn't fighting the case entirely alone. Being employed by the insurance company didn't offer much physical protection, but it was a kind of protection. The company's lawyers, I knew from experience, were connected. They could pull more strings than a harpist.

I got back in the car and headed towards the motorway. Horns sounded left and right in the mid-morning traffic. I inched forwards, through traffic lights and roadworks. People were walking faster than me on the pavements. Trams sped past in the middle of the road, their clatter reminding me how slowly I was moving.

Eventually, I got onto the ring road and sped towards the motorway toll-booths. I watched the lucky drivers speeding through the telepass funnel, the arm rising automatically without them even needing to change down a gear. They sped off into the distance as I queued for one of the manual tickets. There were at least a dozen cars in front of me. I cursed my stupidity in not having a telepass installed in my car. I've often lost track of people I was tailing because I had to queue at the toll booth. It's like trying to race someone with your legs tied together.

The queue inched forward. My feet moved alternately up and down on the pedals like I was pumping an old-fashioned organ. I must have been thinking about organs, about air and traffic flow and what sort of legacy they leave: an organ concerto or a telepass bill. I suddenly stopped the car and pulled on the handbrake. Within seconds the cars behind me were honking, irritated that I had allowed a car's length gap to appear in front of me. I stayed where I was and pulled out my phone. I looked at the snap of Santagata's Fiat. I zoomed in on the windscreen, trying to see if I could see a telepass sensor. The image wasn't clear enough to see that sort of detail. By now cars behind were pulling out and overtaking me, offering me their opinion of my driving skills as they revved past.

I reversed out of there and headed back towards the city. Unless we always walk or whisper or use cash, there's a slipstream of electronic evidence from the gadgets we use: a credit card transaction, a telepass receipt, a log of a call. There's almost no part of our human interaction that isn't mediated by gadgetry, and we've become so used to it that we don't even realise it's an interface any more. We get on with our lives without thinking that where we've been and what we've done can leave some kind of electronic fingerprint or footprint.

After a couple of calls I found the Telepass offices. They were blue and yellow. The colours were everywhere: above the door, on the upholstery, on the front desk. No one was around, so I sat down and read about the company. It was a confident brand, boasting of how it had gone from humble beginnings in 1990 to having over six million users. Like many things, it managed to make me feel out of touch, like I had missed a boat and was left behind. I was still one of the motorway dinosaurs, scratching around for change at the booths where other, more modern drivers sailed through.

I put the pamphlet down as a woman came into the reception area. She, obviously, was wearing the required colours and looked like an Ikea air-hostess.

'Can I help?' she asked.

'I want to talk to the manager,' I said, passing her the usual card.

She looked at it and then back at me. She nodded and went off through a frosted glass door behind her desk.

Eventually another woman came into the waiting room. She was obviously senior enough not to wear the uniform. Her trouser suit was black, as was her perfectly parted short hair. She was attractive in a foreboding kind of way. She held out her slender hand and shook my hand formally whilst her eyes swept round the foyer to make sure it was in order.

'How can I help?'

'Can we talk in private?'

'Certainly.'

She led me through the frosted glass door to her office. It was a small, functional room, surprisingly empty of anything other than a desk and a computer. She went out to get another chair and motioned for me to sit down.

'I need the details on the movement of a car,' I said.

She smiled as if that was what she was asked all the time. 'Jealous spouse?'

'Murder.'

Her smile froze. 'We only give out details to the appropriate authorities with the necessary warrants.'

I straightened my leg, leaning slightly in the chair to pull out my wallet. Before I had even opened it she was shaking her head.

'We don't sell information either.'

'Signora, this is a murder case.'

'I co-operate with the Carabinieri, not with some', she looked at my card, 'so-called private investigator. If it's a murder, why aren't the authorities here?'

'They're not quite so quick.' I smiled.

'I'll wait for them to catch up then.'

She was self-possessed and cold. She was the kind of person who was intriguing because you wanted to discover if they had any warmth inside them. I asked for her name and fax number and went and sat in the car. I phoned Speranza, the man in Milan who was supposed to be investigating the Tosti killing. I brought him up to speed with the case and told him about my suspicions regarding Santagata.

'I need some information about Santagata's movements,' I said slowly. 'I don't even know if he's got a telepass, but even if he does the woman here in the office is a stickler for formality. Won't release any information without the proper requests and so on.'

'Which office?'

'Milano. It's the central telepass place,' I said impatiently.

'You want me to call her?'

'She's the kind of woman who probably won't sneeze without the right piece of paper. A fax might do the trick.'

'You've got a number?'

I read it out to him and he promised to get something over there.

'This morning?' I asked.

'I'll try. I'll get one of my men to type it up now.'

I thanked him and got out of the car. It was one of those Padanian days where there were no clouds but when the sky wasn't truly blue. It was hazy and heavy and the air smelt as fresh as a motorway hard-shoulder.

I walked around the city's suburbs for a while. Everywhere was noisy and hot. I could smell spilt fuel and wet grass and rotting fruit and expensive perfume and chip fat and rosmarino and launderette suds and sweat and tram brakes. Extraordinary faces loomed out of the crowd: faces from other countries and continents who had washed up in this huge, sprawling city. It didn't look like many of them had found their fortune, if that's what they were looking for. Mopeds roared past carrying couples in shiny jackets across the cobbles. My ankle hurt and I stopped to rotate it slowly whilst leaning up against a bus-stop.

Speranza called two hours later. 'We've sent the fax through,' he said. 'You'll keep me informed?'

When I went back into the offices, the receptionist nodded at me like we were old friends.

'Can I see the manager again?' I asked.

She went into the offices behind her desk again. Eventually, she came back and led me into the cool woman's office.

'You're back,' she said, looking at me with surprise.

'You received the fax?'

She nodded, looking at me with curiosity. 'You've obviously got friends in high places.'

'And enemies in low ones.'

She looked at me briefly. 'Have you got the number plate concerned?'

I gave her the plate details, reading the numbers and letters from the snap on my phone. She tapped in the details and then sat back. 'Which period are you interested in?'

I gave her the date of Tosti's killing and watched her shuffling the mouse around, clicking here and there. She tutted, as if to say they had no records.

'Nothing?'

She shook her head. 'It's not a registered vehicle. Anything else?'

'Can you search by name?'

'Certainly.'

I told her to look under Antonio Santagata. She started typing without saying anything. She was quite an iceberg. I heard the sound of her fingertips on the keyboard, like the sound of a train rattling over the tracks. She took the mouse and started clicking again. I shut my eyes and it sounded like the noise of an indicator from the inside of a car. But the result was the same. Nothing came up under that name. No smoking gun. There never is in this country; only the smoke. The smoke and fog and sand. Anything that obscures and confuses and silts up. Nothing's ever conclusive, nothing's ever black and white. Except Tommy and the way he died.

I drove towards the underwear shop where Tosti's widow worked. I heard a child's crying as I walked in and saw Rosaria behind the glass counter. She was bending down to try to reason with what looked liked a furious two-year-old. His nose and eyes were running and his skin was blotchy. I couldn't understand what he was shouting, and neither could his mother, which only made him shout louder.

She straightened up when she saw me. The child saw me too and immediately stopped his screaming.

'What was all that noise for?' I asked him. He slid behind his mother's thigh, his staggered breathing muffled by her trousers.

Rosaria looked at me and rolled her eyes. She smiled and shook her head to show me her exasperation. It felt like a friendly gesture, a hint that she and I were somehow on the same level.

'Any news?' she asked.

I took out my phone, found the snap of Santagata and put it on the glass counter. She picked it up and stared at it. She frowned and shook her head.

'You've never seen him?'

She shook her head again.

'You're sure?'

She was. 'The man who was hassling Luciano was older than that. Thinner.'

It sounded like D'Antoni, the thin, wily local politician. But I doubted that he ever got his hands dirty. I found the recording of Santagata's voice and played that to her. She shook her head again.

I was surprised. I had thought I was on the home straight, but her reaction threw me. It wasn't even a 'maybe.' The boy was pulling at her sleeve now and she turned round to see what he wanted. He whispered something to her whilst staring at me.

Her reaction to the picture of Davide Pace was the same. Nothing. She shrugged and apologised as if it were her fault. She bent down and picked up the boy, groaning slightly as she took his weight. He straddled her hip, resting his head on her shoulder as he looked at me out of the corner of his eye.

As always, I woke up early the next morning. It was just gone four. The flat was freezing. I pulled on socks and a jumper and went to make coffee. I flicked on the light of the extractor fan above the hob because it was more gentle on the eyes and pulled up the tapparelle slowly, hoping not to wake the neighbours. Outside, the street was deserted. I opened the window briefly to enjoy the air: it was fresh and expectant.

I shut the window and heard the coffee hiss its arrival. I poured a slug into a tazzina and stirred in some sugar. I felt impatient, wishing it was already morning so I could get on and crack the case. But there wasn't much to do yet. I sat at the kitchen table and drew circles with my left foot. It cracked as I rotated it, sounding like a car driving slowly over gravel. I rotated it the other way. More cracks, but gentler this time.

There wasn't much to do at this time of day, so I started knocking some frames together: sandwiching the wax foundation between thin, square sticks that I gently nailed in place. I would need a few hundred of these over the spring and summer, as the weather got warmer and the bees needed more storage space.

Whilst I was at it, my mind wandered over the case. I needed to get Davide Pace to sign an affidavit. When it was a decent hour I phoned him and his sad voice came on the line.

I told him what we needed to do, but he began stammering, saying there was no point. I told him I would be round at his house in a quarter of an hour.

I walked through the centre, past the usual adolescents in clothes they had seen on MTV: oversize, bright-coloured baseball tops whose shoulders were at their elbows. They bounced around the steps of the Duomo, trying to disguise their self-consciousness with apeish loudness. A woman with bowed legs was begging outside the Battistero. She had a sign saying 'ho fame'.

The concrete piazza looked even more ugly in daylight. It was grey and the finish was rough. I rang the bell to the Pace apartment and was buzzed in.

He was standing at the door to his flat like he wanted to block me from entering. He looked embarrassed and defiant at the same time.

'I made a mistake,' he whispered as soon as I was level with him.

'It wasn't your fault. You didn't know what Santagata was planning to do. No one will blame you.'

'You don't understand.' He was looking at the floor. 'I got it wrong.'

'Got what wrong?'

He raised his round face to look me in the eyes. He looked strained, like he was lifting weights as well as his eyes. He was breathing heavily. 'I made a mistake. I didn't ever give any petrol to anyone.'

It sounded like he was repeating someone else's words and I told him so. He just looked at me as if pleading for me to understand.

'Those petrol cans that you bought have been found in a skip outside Santagata's apartment. You bought them, he disposed of them. If you start obstructing justice, you're an accessory and the Carabinieri will be here instead of me. An accessory to manslaughter.'

He repeated his line. 'I didn't ever give any petrol to anyone.'

'A boy died,' I said. 'Lost his life. Do you understand that? You effectively bought the murder weapon.'

He was staring at the floor showing me only his thinning hair.

'I think', I whispered, 'that you were a good Samaritan. You did him the kind of favour any friend would do.'

His head sprang up like I had removed the weights.

'But if you start telling lies and siding with him, you're in trouble. Real trouble. There are records of what went on. Phone records, receipts, fingerprints. And you start to look like an accessory.'

He just repeated his favourite sentence again. I interrupted him and told him what sort of man I thought he was. I walked back down the corridor swearing to myself about cowardice and coglioni. I was about to limp down the steps when a thought occurred to me. I turned round and walked back along the corridor. By now his door was shut and I rang the bell.

'Cosa?' he said with fatigue as he opened the door a crack.

'Where's he from?'

'Who?'

'Santagata. Where's he from originally?'

He looked down the corridor before answering, to make

sure no one was there. The boy was more paranoid than I thought. 'Monteleccio,' he said quickly, shutting the door again as if it could keep away his worries.

The town of Monteleccio was an hour and a half south of the city at the far end of the province. The road there was straight at first, going through various towns and villages whose names I remembered from summer fairs long ago. But for the last half-hour the road zig-zagged up into the mountains and clouds. Everywhere suddenly looked different: bleaker, braver, more solid. The people by the roadside looked sterner and stronger, dressed for survival rather than for fashion.

The town had only one central square, though it wasn't particularly square. It was built on a slope and had a small monument in the middle. A church stood on the higher side of the square whilst a bar, with an old-fashioned lantern on the outside, was at the lower end. I let gravity pull me towards the bar.

It was warm and noisy inside. I could hear guttural shouts and laughter. Men who hadn't shaved for days sat around tables playing cards. The chairs were three deep around one game and most of the men had small glasses of grappa in their fists. The only woman in there was behind the bar.

'Salve.' She smiled at me.

'Coffee please.'

'Subito.'

She set about the usual ritual and I looked around the bar. None of the men had even noticed I had come in. She put the coffee in front of me and moved away to serve someone else.

I looked to the end of the bar and saw a man who was a good twenty years younger than the others. He said something to me that I didn't understand. I shuffled towards him and asked him to repeat it. It was something about the weather, but his accent was still incomprehensible.

We both stared ahead, sinking our coffees. I caught a glimpse of his face in the mirror behind the bar and his eyes looked bloodshot, as if he had had too much drink or cold air or both. He had thick black curly hair and the kind of pinched face that suggested he would be loyal to whoever treated him worst.

'I'm from Milan,' I said. 'I've come back to try and find old relatives who might still be living here.'

He looked me up and down like he had never seen someone from the city. 'Ah sì?'

'My grandfather left this town after the war. He always told me about his brothers here.'

'Which family?' He asked the question like he might have something to gain from the encounter, like I might have untold riches to hand out to the hardened montanari.

'D'Antoni.'

'D'Antoni?' he repeated. He shook his head. 'I've been here forty years and never heard of a D'Antoni.'

I frowned as if I were surprised. In truth I wasn't. It had been a long shot, but one worth trying. I knew Luciano Tosti had come from here. This was where he had met his wife. And if he and D'Antoni had been from the same place I would have a connection.

'You could talk to one of the older men.'

He shouted to one of the men on the fringes of the card game. A man in a red and grey jumper came towards us slightly unsteadily. It looked like he had been here drinking since breakfast. His wiry, unbrushed hair and blackened teeth suggested it might have been longer.

My friend introduced us and explained that I was trying to trace my ancestors. The man shook his head silently whilst staring at me. The gesture made me think that the wily man knew I was lying.

'Never heard of a D'Antoni round these parts,' he said.

'Sure you've got the right town?' the younger man asked.

'Monteleccio? Absolutely. My grandfather spoke about it often enough. Told us all about his friends. There was a family called Tosti I remember.'

'Was,' said the older man. 'They left a while back.'

We had common ground at least and I decided to try out a few more names just for luck. 'He told me about the Santagatas,' I nodded, underlining my reliability.

'I'm a Santagata,' the old man said, smiling broadly. 'What did he tell you about us, eh?'

'You are?' I said, letting it sink in. He held out his hand and I shook it.

'What did he say about us?'

I made up some story about how a Santagata had stolen my grandfather's sweetheart. The man drank it up like it was grappa. He grinned and said that success with women was in the genes. He asked the barmaid for confirmation and she looked at him with affection and nodded. The man ordered a grappa for me and started telling anyone who would listen about how rumours of his family's powers of seduction had reached Milan. A few people laughed and turned round to look at us. I raised my glass and threw it back.

'And wasn't there a family called Moroni?'

'Sure. Still is.' The man pointed at one of the card players sitting at the table. 'There are more Moronis in this village than we know what to do with.'

The rush of scorching alcohol fuelled my euphoria. I had known Tosti and Santagata were from up here, but Moroni had come as a surprise. They were all from this same small town. Moroni must have gone back to his roots when looking for people to do his dirty work. It made sense in a strange, subtle way. People always go close to home when looking for prestanomi, the frontmen who pretend to be the owners of a flat or a bank account. When Moroni wanted muscle or a frontman, he went back to Monteleccio.

I slapped some coins on the counter and walked out. The hairpins seemed tighter on the drive back to the city, perhaps because both car and blood were moving faster. I was in the city in little over an hour. Near the pavement where I parked I saw one of those walls where political campaigners had pasted up election posters. Every poster had the face of the aspiring politician. There was no originality, no humour, nothing other than a huge close-up of their mug with, underneath, their vacuous promises: 'working for you' or 'solidarity and good sense'. I walked further along the wall and saw the Italia Fiera poster: 'proud to be proud' it said. I looked at D'Antoni's face. The poster was peeling away at the edges but it was clearly him. He looked like a benign, fit grandfather in the photograph. I took hold of one brittle corner of the poster and ripped a strip off. 'Proud eh?' I asked the mute photograph as I screwed up the strip.

I decided to go and see Bragantini one last time. I drove round to the factory but it was deserted. The only thing still in the car park was the burnt-out shell of his old Audi, the thing that had lit the fuse of this case in the first place. I looked at it there, inert and innocent.

There was nobody around. I phoned Bragantini and he told me he was at home. I walked round and he came to the door in casual clothes. He looked incongruous in jumper and jeans, as if he had lost his old identity and was trying out a new one. He welcomed me inside like he didn't have a care in the world.

He led me into his study, talking over his shoulder as he went. 'You're here to give me an invoice, I take it?'

'Not really.'

He stopped and turned round. His face looked more severe. 'What are you doing here then?'

'Just a couple of final questions.'

He made a disgruntled growl.

'Your insurance company has employed me to look into the circumstances surrounding the fire.'

He looked at me quizzically. 'That's ridiculous.' His good humour evaporated.

'They've asked me to treat you as a suspect, just like everyone else.'

He told me where to go and what to do once I got there.

I smiled and batted away the insult with the back of my hand. 'I know you're not a suspect. You're the victim in this. I know that.'

He looked up at me, surprised, I assumed, by my support. I repeated what I had said, to make sure he knew I was on his side.

'I'm sorry,' he said, sitting down and holding his forehead in his hands. He sat there like that for a while, rubbing the balls of his thumbs into his temples. 'I just want my life back.' He took his hands away and looked at me over his shoulder. 'I was a successful businessman. Never knowingly wronged anyone. Worst I ever did was drive a hard bargain. And now I find my factory burnt to the ground and I'm despised across the city. Treated like a criminal.'

I nodded. We sat like that for a few minutes. A woman in an old-fashioned domestic's apron came in, saw us sitting there like pensive mourners, and walked out again.

'Was that Valentina?'

He nodded. 'How did you know?'

'I spoke to her about something. In her own way, she broke the case open for me.'

'Valentina?' He sounded incredulous.

I told him briefly about the restaurants, about how Valentina always left his home number when she reserved a table. I told him that someone had been watching him and had followed him into Il Cucchiaio a couple of weeks ago to get his number from the bookings.

'Bastardi,' he said to himself.

'Spying on you for weeks probably.'

He shook his head aggressively. I was glad to see some of his old anger coming back. I wanted to needle one last piece of information from him.

'Who are you selling to?'

'There's some cordata.' He waved his fingers in the air like he didn't care about anything any more.

It was a word I disliked. There's always some cordata. It meant originally a bunch of climbers all roped – corded – together. But now it means a consortium, a bunch of people who have grouped together to climb to the top of the capitalist peak.

'What are they called?'

He looked at me and hesitated. He must have known if he gave me a name I might manage to sabotage his sale. 'It's an Ati,' he said quietly and with contempt.

'What's that?'

'Associazione temporanea d'imprese.'

'Meaning?'

'Meaning you have absolutely no idea who's involved. It's an association that guarantees complete privacy to the participants.' He rolled his eyes. 'There's no register of who's involved, no record of the percentages of participation. All I know is the price they're prepared to pay.'

'And you're happy with it?'

He shook his head. 'I'm not happy at all, but I've got no choice. You know that the insurance company's hardly likely to pay out if it's proved to be arson anyway. I've got to take what I can get.'

'From whoever you can get it?'

He stared at the ceiling as if imploring it for patience.

'Ci vediamo,' I said, bouncing my fist gently on his shoulder as I went out.

I was walking home when I suddenly realised my phone was ringing. I pulled it out and heard an unfamiliar voice. It was some farmer who said he had got my number from the beekeepers' association. He had a swarm of bees in the corner of one of his fields.

I didn't really want the distraction but I knew, from experience, that it can help. Sometimes the bees take your mind off the case and force you to concentrate on something else.

The farm was a few miles outside the city. The swarm was hanging from the branch of a tree like a throbbing, humming lump of dark mud the shape of an elongated football. The air was thick with little black dots, flying noisily in search of somewhere more permanent. Up close you could see that the amorphous lump was made up of tens of thousands of insects. The noise was loud, a sort of hypnotic drone. The farmer stood a good way back, watching with curiosity as I laid a large sheet on the ground.

Taking a swarm is one of the easiest aspects of beekeeping. It's mechanical more than anything else. I shook the branch hard and the majority of the blob fell into my yellow straw skep. I broke off a few of the smaller branches and tried to throw the bees off them into the skep as well. Some fell off, some stayed where they were.

When the skep was full of the black mass, I upended it over the sheet. I propped up one edge with a spare brick so that there was a thin opening. Within a few minutes I could see some of the bees with their abdomens in the air, fanning away to communicate that this skep was the new home and everyone should get inside. Slowly I watched as thousands of noisy dots crawled up under the thing.

'I'll leave it here a while, give them time to settle. I'll pick it up later,' I said to the farmer.

He took half a step closer now to look at the sheet and the skep. He leant forward like he was looking over a cliff and nodded. I looked at him. His face was rust-coloured with grey stubble across the chin. His thick hair was dull and matt, like it was washed with ash. He was the sort of man that spoke in monosyllables, and even then only when necessary.

He stepped back and looked at me. 'Drink?'

I nodded, trying to imitate his reticence, and followed him to a barn the other end of the field. Inside the barn two rows of cows were munching on hay thrown out in a central aisle. A couple raised their heads to look at us and mooed a greeting. We walked through the middle to a far corner. The farmer moved bits of hose and wire from a dusty shelf and found an unlabelled bottle. He poured two shots into two small glasses that looked like they hadn't been cleaned for a year or two. He passed me mine without saying anything and we clinked and threw them back. It was the kind of grappa that had no flavour, only a cruel afterburn. He was already pouring two more shots. We clinked again and threw them back.

The drink loosened his tongue a fraction. He asked the usual questions about beekeeping's yields and costs, listening to the replies as he stared into the distance, like he was calculating the tiny profit margins. I told him it was just a hobby and he looked me up and down like I was one of his livestock that hadn't fattened up sufficiently.

As he put the bottle back on the shelf something that looked like a power drill caught my eye. The end of it was slightly swollen, like the nozzle that holds a drill bit, but otherwise it looked like a pistol: a similar trigger and butt.

'What's that?'

He followed my eyes and picked up the drill. 'Captive bolt pistol,' he said.

He passed it over and I took its unexpected weight. I watched the farmer walk over to one of his cows and put his fingers to its large, flat forehead. He suddenly pulled his hand up as if from a recoil.

'Knocks them unconscious,' he walked back towards me, 'so their heart is still pumping as you bleed them.'

'Merda,' I said to myself.

'It's very humane,' he said in self-defence.

I swore again under my breath. I quickly thanked him and told him I would be back for the swarm in the evening. I ran to the car, feeling my ankle struggling to hold up on the uneven terrain. I revved the engine and sped towards the motorway.

I hoped it wasn't true, but it felt true. It had the shocking, unexpected feel of a truth that transformed everything. It should have been obvious. The man's anger, his tirades against the profiteers, his admission that he kept the animals himself. I had been so focused on the heavyweights that I had missed the minnow in front of my eyes. The sort of lightweight who had snapped, had suddenly decided that it was his turn to impersonate the powerful.

The telepass offices were about to close when I got there. The woman on the front desk stood up as I stormed through her space and into the manager's office.

'I got the wrong name,' I said.

The iceberg manager looked at me with curiosity.

'Run another check for me, will you?'

The receptionist had caught up with me now and was looking at her boss apologetically. She was dismissed with a brusque tilt of lacquered hair.

'Allora?' the woman said, trying to restore order.

'Carlo Lombardi. Resident in Parma. Check for 12 March last year.'

She tapped away and I watched her. 'We've got a lot of Lombardis. Got anything more specific?'

I came round behind her and looked at the screen. There was a whole page of them. I took the mouse out of her hand and clicked on one after the other until I found the one I was looking for. I brought it up on screen and moved away, letting her take over again.

'12 March last year,' I said.

She clicked and typed and eventually I heard the printer whirring and watched a solitary sheet of paper emerge.

'Prego,' she said with pointed politeness.

I walked over to the printer and picked up the piece of paper. I stared at it, knowing that I had found my smoking gun. Lombardi had been in Milan the night Luciano Tosti was murdered. I felt more sadness than ecstasy.

The drive to Carla's lingerie shop was slow. There were

traffic lights on every block and roadworks on every other. Impatient drivers played chicken with oncoming trams whilst others who knew the city better than me peeled off onto narrow sidestreets.

When I got to the shop I saw Rosaria. She was serving a customer and had three open boxes on the counter. The customer was picking up garments one after the other and inspecting them carefully. Rosaria saw me and nodded. The customer left without buying anything.

'You like prosciutto?' I asked Rosaria.

'I'm a vegetarian.'

'Well, we're going to go and buy some crudo anyway.'

'I'm working.'

'Call your friend. We've got to go. Now.'

She looked at me for an instant and then walked off through the back door. She came back with the old lady who was holding the young boy. We left without saying anything. We heard the boy screaming for his mother as we got in the car.

We drove back to Parma in silence. She must have known what was happening and her face looked determined, set against the world. An hour or so later I parked up outside the familiar prosciuttificio.

'I want you to go in there and just order an etto of the stuff. Here.' I passed her a fiver.

'Who's in there?'

'You tell me.'

'You think it's the man who killed Luciano?'

I nodded.

'What if he recognises me?'

'He won't.'

'He might know what I'm doing. Might realise . . .'

I reassured her. Told her to go in when other customers were in there, told her I would go in ten seconds after her.

She stared out of the windscreen for a minute, breathing heavily as she prepared to meet the man who had killed her husband. We watched a couple go in and she opened the car door and went in after them.

She came back out within a few seconds. Her hand was over her face and she was bent double as she walked.

I got out and opened her door for her. She held on to me, clinging to my shoulders as if she was about to collapse completely. 'He's the one,' she said, 'the one who came round to our flat and was shouting at Luciano.'

It didn't mean he had necessarily done anything more than that, but it didn't look good. I lowered her into the car and told her I would be back in a minute. I saw the couple coming out of the shop and held the door open for them before going in myself.

'Detective,' he said cheerfully as I came in.

'Buongiorno,' I said, formally.

'What can I get you?'

'Is there somewhere we can talk?' I asked.

He looked at me sideways. 'Sure.' He crabbed to the side door behind the counter and called his wife. He hung his white coat on the back of the door and came round the front. He put his hand inside my elbow, the way some older men do round here, and walked me towards the front door.

'Let's go outside,' he said. 'I need a cigarette.'

'Sure.'

He let a couple of customers come in, holding the door open for them. 'Salve, salve,' he said, bowing slightly with the deference of the eager retailer.

Outside, we stood with our backs to the warehouse. He lit the cigarette and then turned to me. 'Any closer to finding your arsonist?'

I shrugged. 'I found him.'

'Really?'

I nodded. 'I know who it is. I know why and how. But the authorities don't want to know.'

'It's all about profits.' He waved his cigarette in the direction of the cranes a few hundred metres away. 'What's a human life compared to a healthy bank balance? If they want to build, they won't let anything stand in their way. Not you, not me. They're ruthless bastards.'

'So you fight fire with fire?'

'How do you mean?'

'Someone had to take a stand. You took it. You stood up for yourself.'

He turned and squinted at me, trying to understand what I was talking about.

'The thing I've noticed', I said, watching the cranes turning slowly, 'is that sometimes indignation makes us do things just as bad as what made us indignant in the first place.'

'What are you talking about?' He asked the question with a fraction of aggression.

'I'm talking about Luciano Tosti.'

He was staring ahead. He didn't say anything, but pulled hard on his cigarette. I watched the orange end speed towards his mouth as he sucked in. He exhaled slowly and turned towards me. He didn't say anything, just stared at me. I watched his face melt from defiance to confusion. He turned away again and took a last drag on his cigarette. He flicked the butt towards the car park.

'That man took away everything I had ever worked for. A lifetime spent building up a business and he took it all away from me.'

'He didn't exactly take it. He bought it.'

'He bought it with threats. Burning my car, threatening my family. He bought it cheap, got planning permission and sold it at a huge profit. He deserved everything he got.'

'What did he get?'

'He got what was coming to him.'

'A blow to the brain? Slaughtered like one of your pigs?'

I looked at Lombardi, who was still staring ahead. If he felt any remorse, he was hiding it pretty well. His face was set against the world, his mouth rigid as he breathed noisily through his nostrils. Eventually he turned towards me.

'How did you know?' he asked softly.

'A guess. I saw a captive bolt pistol earlier on today. Just by chance. The sort used to stun livestock. The mark it leaves looks like a hammer blow to the untrained eye. Hit the temple in the right place and you can kill a man. And then I realised that you seemed more angry about Tosti than anyone else. I didn't want to believe it, so I went to the telepass offices and got your records. You were in Milan the night he was killed.'

He closed his eyes.

'I saw that you had driven to Milan and back that night, which was coincidental. So I spoke to Tosti's widow again. She had already told me her late husband had been harassed

257

in the weeks before his death. I asked her to come to your prosciuttificio just now and identify you.'

He grunted. 'That's who she was. I knew her from somewhere. I knew her face.'

'And she knew yours. Said she was certain you were the person who had come to see her husband in the week before the murder.'

He was nodding slowly. 'I had gone to confront him, to make sure he knew what he had done to me and my family. And he treated me like dirt. Insulted me as if I were some useless idiot who deserved what he got.' He growled at the memory of it.

'So you went back a few days later?'

'I hadn't intended to shoot him. I wanted to scare him. That's why I didn't even think about the trail I was leaving, about the telepass data or even making sure I wasn't seen. I just wanted to take out the pistol and wave it in his face. I wanted to make him weep and beg. Make him say sorry, that was all. I never intended to kill him.'

'But?'

'He was the same as before. He stopped for the cancello to open and even when he saw the gun he laughed. Called me a sfigato and was about to speed off down the ramp. I clenched my fists in anger. It was instinctive. And of course the thing went off. He had been laughing at me and then he just stopped. He just', there was a quiver in his voice as he repeated it, 'stopped.'

His voice was trembling as he spoke. I turned to look at him but he was still staring resolutely ahead as if I weren't there.

We stood there for a few minutes. I listened to the sound of a distant, mechanical hammer, a rhythmic reminder of the relentless building. The cranes were gyrating a few hundred metres away, their triangular metal arms turning towards and away from each other as if in a slow-motion courting ritual.

'What happens now?' he asked. His voice was almost childish. He sounded bewildered.

'You turn yourself in. You tell the authorities what you told me.'

He sighed heavily as I spoke.

'Take a lawyer with you.'

'They'll put me away for twenty years. My grandchildren will be grown-up by the time I'm out.' He was talking to himself as if I wasn't there. 'My wife can't run this place on her own. She won't survive. She'll . . .' He screwed his face up. His shoulders bounced and he slid down the wall until he was sitting on the floor, his legs twisted beneath him.

'I'll call your wife,' I said, looking at him briefly before going inside.

She was there at the counter, wiping the surfaces. She looked up at me and must have sensed I was there to bring bad news.

'Where's Carlo?' she said quickly.

'Outside.'

'What's happened?'

'Go and talk to him.'

'What's happened?' she said again. 'Is he OK?'

She followed me outside and saw him slumped on the floor. She ran over to him and knelt down. I didn't hear what they said, but heard her moan and saw her collapse to the floor beside him.

I walked away and pulled out my phone.

'Speranza?' I said as the gruff voice came on the line. 'It's Castagnetti. I've got your man.'

He asked for an explanation and I told him the outline. He barely even remembered who Carlo Lombardi was. Said he had only ever seen a captive bolt pistol in some film a while back. He said he would send a local unit round to pick him up.

I went back and sat in the car next to Rosaria. When she looked at me her eyes were red. There was a screwed-up tissue in her hands. We sat there in silence for a few minutes. I kept an eye on Lombardi, slumped against the wall of his warehouse. Within a few minutes the Carabinieri arrived and his wife started wailing and beating her chest as Lombardi was lifted and bundled into their car.

'There's someone I want you to meet,' I said to Rosaria. She didn't reply so I put the car in gear and drove towards the part of town where I had met François under the bridge. I tried to explain to Rosaria what we were doing, but I barely knew myself.

'You said', I started, 'that you didn't know what to do with the money your husband made on that land deal. Didn't know who to give it to.' I told her about Tommy's death, told her how it came about because of the same crew that had manipulated her husband and infuriated Lombardi. I tried to persuade her there was some connection. She didn't say anything, just listened.

I parked the car outside the bar where we had taken a

coffee a while back. We walked across the lumpy no-man's land towards the archway. The heavy blankets were still there, and we could smell woodsmoke as we got closer.

'Permesso,' I said out of habit as I pulled back the blanket.

There were the same hollow faces as before. People struggling to survive against the cold and the hunger. I saw Rosaria taking it all in and it looked as if she were about to break down again.

'I'm looking for François,' I said.

Someone thumbed over their shoulder to the far side of the archway. We stepped over empty cans and sodden plastic bags and I saw him sitting up in his sleeping bag.

'Ciao Mister,' he said enthusiastically.

'You hungry?'

He nodded eagerly and stood up. We went back to the same bar we had gone to before. He made Rosaria smile wistfully. She kept asking him questions with a combination of curiosity and pity. They seemed to have an immediate connection and I decided to leave them there together. They already looked close, almost thrown into intimacy by a shared sorrow. I wondered, if I ever saw them again, if they would have become mother and son.

'You want a lift back home?' I asked her.

'I'll hang around here for a while. I'll get the train back.'

I raised a hand by way of goodbye, and they both nodded back, Rosaria raising a hand which stayed there in the air as if there was still so much to say.

I sat in the car feeling drained and disorientated. I had thought Carlo Lombardi was one of life's good guys and, in a way, he was. He had done what he had because he was pushed to the limit by systematic malfeasance, by a sense that there was no other way to defend himself. He had seen his life's work stolen from him by a mixture of threats and arson and sleight of hand and he wanted an apology. When he didn't even get that, he went, in a moment of madness, for retribution.

The tragedy was that he had merely targeted the weakest link. He had gone for the public face of the scam and the public face is always the least powerful of all the players. Tosti was nothing more than a pawn, a man who was put up to the job. He only gained what he did by trying to squeeze a better deal for his family.

An hour later, I got a phone call from a voice I half recognised. He said his name was Cesare Carini. It rang a distant bell.

'You left your card in my letter box a few days ago,' he said.

'Investimenti Emiliani?'

'Exactly.'

He was the man who had lent Tosti the money a year ago. The man who hadn't opened his door to me.

'I apologise if I was discourteous the other day.' His voice sounded melliflous, not a quality I usually trusted in this land of smooth talkers.

'I don't mind discourtesy,' I said. 'You know where you stand with discourtesy. It's courtesy I find unreliable.'

'Quite.' There was a brief pause. 'I've got something you might be interested in.'

'What?'

'I was recently invited to join an ATI. You know what an ATI is?'

This country has more acronyms than humans. At least Bragantini had already explained it to me. 'A temporary association of companies.'

'Indeed,' the voice said formally. 'I declined the invitation.'

'Why?'

'Because the costs are too high. I heard about the death of that African boy. Last year my name was dragged into the investigation into the death of Luciano Tosti. However high the returns are, I didn't want to be part of that sort of association.'

'So why are you calling me?'

'Because I thought you might like to know the participants.'

I reached for a pen quickly and pulled a piece of paper towards me.

'The mandataria – you're familiar with that term? It implies the senior partner in the enterprise – is Masi Costruzione. The mandanti, the junior partners, are the following. You have a pen? Good.' He drew breath and then rattled them off as I scribbled down the names: 'CGB Holdings. Picem Srl. TT Systems Srl. Lucana Enterprises Spa. You want the percentages?'

'Why are you telling me this?'

'Because I'm an honest banker. These people appear to be profiting from human sacrifice.'

It sounded noble but he must have had another motive. Perhaps he wanted revenge on people who had dragged his name into a murder investigation.

'And who are these people?'

'It's not hard to find out. You're the detective aren't you? Buon lavoro.'

The line went dead. I stared at the names I had scribbled down and then at the telephone. I went round to the Camera di Commercio, the local Companies House. It was almost closing time and the man wasn't enthusiastic about being waylaid. With a bit of encouragement he eventually brought up the details of the companies involved.

It was like percentages within percentages. There were

individuals – Beatrice Bravi, Alessandro Santucci, Massimo Matteucci, Bruno Santagata – who owned percentages of certain companies. And those companies were then part of a 'temporary association' of companies, each with their own percentage of participation. The whole thing could go on indefinitely. That temporary association could then become part of a larger association, or those individuals might themselves be only fronts for other people, in which case their percentages of the companies within the association would be divided amongst the people they were fronting up for. My head was spinning. It was as if a rich cake had been reduced to crumbs and suddenly so many people were tucking in that none of it made sense any more.

I called Giacomo, the die-hard left-wing politician I had seen at the rally the day after Tommy's death. He, more than anyone, was likely to know who the people behind the cordata were.

We met in an unfashionable bar outside the Cittadella with large blue and yellow flags flying from above the awning. It had a cold, bare back room where we could talk. I took out my piece of paper and read him the names one by one.

'Massimo Matteucci,' I said.

He nodded. 'He's the provincial head of some bank. Can't remember which one. A major contributor to Italia Fiera locally.'

I smiled bitterly and looked down at my list. 'Alessandro Santucci.'

'Santucci? Don't know him. Might be a relative of the senator. You know Gherardo Santucci?'

'Beatrice Bravi.'

'Beatrice? She's the daughter of . . .' He stopped himself. 'Have these people done something wrong?'

'They're just part of a consortium. They're investors in a business. Who is she?'

'She's the daughter of a colleague.'

'On your side of the fence?'

'Sure. You've heard of Michele Bravi. He was there at the rally the other night. He was as incensed about the whole white death as anyone.'

'Yeah, I bet he was. He wanted to pressure Bragantini so his daughter could snap up the land. She's one of the biggest investors in this whole scam.'

He was shaking his head. He pushed his thumb and finger under his glasses and rubbed his eyes, his glasses bouncing on his forehead as he did so. He adjusted them again and shook his head. 'Who else?'

I went through the other names and he told me what he knew. There was the owner of the local TV station. Someone from the board of the football team who was close to D'Antoni. One of the largest shareholders of the local paper.

By the time we had finished I felt like steam was coming out of my ears. Half a dozen of the city's finest had come together to double their money. They couldn't lose and they must have known they couldn't lose. By the time the next piano regolatore was published they could sell to whoever they wanted at double or treble the price. It was a stitch-up and what really incensed me was the fact that the cordata was what they call trasversale. It would have been bad enough if D'Antoni had just been using the system to pay back his donors and sponsors and allies, but other parties were involved. The daughter of one of the leading left-wing politicians was in on it as if politics was nothing other than a charade, a little show put on at elections to pretend the electorate had some sort of choice. All that stoked indignation at the death of a poor immigrant was nothing more than a way to put pressure on Bragantini to make sure his little girl made some quick cash. The whole thing disgusted me and the worst of it was that the media would never report the story because the owners of the local rag and the local TV station were in on the deal.

I went round to see Dall'Aglio in the Questura. I wanted to make sure the case wouldn't be shut down, everything neatly tied up and any loose ends simply archived. I was ushered in immediately and welcomed with unusual warmth.

'It's quite a case you've got here Castagnetti,' he said, coming round his desk to offer me his hand.

'You've heard the latest then?' I asked wearily.

'I heard.' He looked at me and bowed minimally. 'For once, you've actually made us look good. My colleagues in Milan are on their way here right now and they're full of praise for the professionalism of this city.'

I rolled my eyes.

'Sit down. Sit down.' He went back behind his desk. 'I thought you said this whole case was political?'

'It is.'

He shook his head like he knew more about it than me. 'It was just the usual disagreement between two private parties. Someone thought he had been ripped off and lost his cool. Took revenge. End of story.'

'Not quite,' I said. 'Tosti wasn't the only one to lose his life. What about Mbora, the lad who died in the fire?'

'We're working on it,' he said distractedly.

'What does that mean?'

He must have felt my anger, because he shuffled paper on

his desk. 'We've got prints from those petrol cans. Both Pace and Santagata have had their hands all over them. We pulled in that girl from the petrol station who gave us a positive ID on Pace from the night of the fire.'

He looked at me like he had done it all by himself and was expecting a pat on the back. I nodded, staring at the ground as I thought about Gaia. If she was the key to the prosecution case, she was in a dangerous position.

'The trouble is', he said, 'there's nothing illegal about buying petrol. We've no proof Santagata used it for what we think he did.'

I growled with impatience. 'Santagata's nephew is part of the cordata trying to buy Bragantini's land.'

He bounced his head slowly, like he was weighing it up.

'And Santagata', I went on, 'is from the same small village up in the mountains as Moroni.' I stared at him and saw him closing his eyes. 'Moroni?' I asked, in case he had forgotten. 'He's the cowboy who muscled his way into the Masi operation. You know who else was from that village?' He didn't say anything. 'Luciano Tosti.'

He sighed heavily, like he was growing tired of my insistence.

'There was a design to this whole operation. Two fires within a week don't happen just by chance. Bragantini even got intimidating phone calls. He reported them, right?'

Dall'Aglio looked down at a corner of his desk, flicking his thumbs outwards like it wouldn't make much difference. The gesture couldn't have been more eloquent if he had shrugged his shoulders.

'You can't *not* make the connections.' I was raising my

269

voice unintentionally. 'Paolo D'Antoni is the assessore all'urbanistica. He knew which land was about to be redesignated. He knew which land was ripe for the picking. He couldn't buy it himself so he started tipping off Moroni in return for his wife getting the contract to sell the flats a few years down the line.'

Dall'Aglio by now was looking pained, like he didn't want to hear it.

'The only trouble was that 3 per cent was only good if it was 3 per cent of something. Three per cent of nothing's not worth much. And with the housing market collapsing and flats not selling, he wasn't happy with his wife's commission. Things were going unsold and his family wasn't making the cash. So he makes sure his wife gets a penthouse on the cheap as well. That way everyone was happy. The politician's family gets thanked properly for the tip-off. The cordata that buys the agricultural land makes a nice profit when the magic wand turns it residential. The constructors make a tidy sum. The only losers are the people who get forced off their land. And the city in general, as we watch another green space disappear under concrete for evermore.'

'Proof?' Dall'Aglio said sharply.

'D'Antoni's wife is given the contract. She's given the flat.'

'Nothing illegal there.'

'Moroni and D'Antoni are business partners. I saw them chatting merrily just a few hours ago.' My voice was rising again and I could feel myself leaning forward as I spoke in an effort to force Dall'Aglio to see it. 'A young man lost his life because of this scam.' I was slicing the air with the palm of my hand in frustration. 'He was burnt alive by a bunch of crooks who were only interested in making more money, so they could buy more cars or votes or whores. That boy was the victim of this whole, orchestrated operation and Paolo D'Antoni is director of the orchestra.'

He raised his fingers to try and calm me down. He looked at me and nodded slowly again. 'What you're saying might be right. Sadly, it sounds plausible. But one can't proceed without proof, without evidence. There's nothing illegal about two grown men having a meal together. Nothing illegal about a politician's wife being given a contract.'

I growled loudly.

'The trouble is,' he said gently, trying to get me on his side, 'we can know full well what's going on, we can be convinced we know the story, but we have to persuade other people. And suspicions aren't very persuasive. And these people are too sharp to leave facts lying around. They know the law better than we do. They don't even commit a crime, not in their eyes. They're just businessmen getting on with business. Prove a link between Santagata and D'Antoni and you might be on to something, but do you really think a fox like D'Antoni is going to be connected to a thug like that?' He shook his head.

'What about phone intercepts?'

He snorted. 'Intercepts? Politicians in Rome are doing everything they can to make them illegal.' He laughed bitterly. 'For years they've been just about the only way we could snare people and now they want to take that away. But even if you get authorisation and actually set up a wiretap, you'll find they talk in code and the courts don't want to learn the language. When these people ask if the tide has come in, what

271

they really mean is whether an illegal package has arrived. You hear them talking about the quality of a horse, they're talking about the purity of the product. They say they want a problem to go away, they mean they want someone sent to eternity. Everything's in code, and it's not enough to know the code, you have to persuade a court that you know the code, and that the people on trial know the code, and then you've got to teach the court the code. And, normally, it only takes a fresh-faced lawyer to plead that everything's a whole lot simpler, that his clients really were just talking about the tide, or a stallion, or a little problem that's now gone away. And the court sighs in relief, because that interpretation is a whole lot easier, and they dismiss the case. The crims end up looking as innocent as new-born lambs. That's just the way it is.' He looked at me with what seemed like sincere condolence. 'I'm sorry.'

I walked out and immediately phoned an acquaintance who worked on the local paper. He had helped me on a case a while back and I owed him a scoop. When I got put through to him I told him the outline, without giving him any names. He whistled and said 'merda' a few times.

'You got anything to back it up?' he asked once I was finished.

I took him through what we had but he was even less impressed than Dall'Aglio. 'Listen, Casta,' he said quickly. I could hear phones constantly ringing in his office. 'You know what they used to do to journalists in the old days? A simple bullet to the temple. Remember Pecorelli? They don't do that any more because it looks bad. So nowadays they start a libel case. A case for a few million euros. Any investigative journalist is bankrupted before they've even hit their thirties. Either that, or editors have all the courage of rabbits in the headlights.'

I tried to persuade him, but he sounded dubious. 'I'll try, of course I'll try. But I've got to say, it's more likely we'll be running a story about this summer's bikini styles.'

The walk home was depressing. I doubted that anyone, other than Lombardi, would ever pay. Santagata might spend a few nights behind bars, but if Davide Pace refused to testify, there was hardly much evidence against him. A couple of cans of petrol outside his house was hardly grounds for a manslaughter charge. I knew what had happened, but a court would want a lot more than that. Even if he did get charged, he would be suicided long before he could involve one of the city's most important politicians in the scam. D'Antoni certainly wouldn't get dragged into it at all. Even though his wife was creaming off the profits from selling flats. Even though he was connected to Moroni and, through him, to Santagata and Tosti. D'Antoni would stay where he was, no doubt about that. He would probably be mayor this time next year.

I twisted the key in the ignition and headed back to the farm where I had left the swarm. By now the place was calmer. There were a few bees around the entrance to the skep, but the majority were quietly inside. I took away the brick and let the skep fall flush with the ground. I took the four corners of the sheet and threw them over the skep, tying them together so that the bees were closed inside and I could carry the whole bundle by the knotted corners. I put it in the boot of the car.

The farmer was watching me with curiosity. I went over to thank him for this new colony and promised to bring him a pot of honey at the end of the summer.

I drove over to Mauro's place. He was coming out of his garage as I opened the boot. He watched me pulling out the sheet and must have heard the loud hum of the swarm inside.

'That's not what I think it is, is it?' he said, walking towards me.

I nodded apologetically. 'You've got room haven't you?'

He shook his head, pretending to be dismayed, but I could see him smiling as I pulled on my veil and gloves. We walked to the far end of the garden where I had an old nucleus hive. I found a plank of plywood in the hedge and rested it up against the entrance. Mauro took a step back as I untied the knot. I upended the skep and beat the side of it hard against my hand so that most of the bees were thrown out onto the plywood. Before long there was a river of them, a living, furry river flowing uphill towards the tiny slit at the base of the hive. It looked so beautiful, their dark, shiny, dangerous bodies all communicating to each other through pitch and position and scent. It was a magnificent ensemble. Some of them stood by the entrance, fanning their pheromones to tell the others that this was now home.

'That girl you asked me to keep an eye on . . .' Mauro said. 'Gaia?'

'She's quite a woman. She realised I was keeping an eye on her and stormed up to the car and started banging on the window, insulting me and saying she wouldn't be intimidated by criminals.' He laughed at the memory. 'I told her you had asked me to look out for her, just check she was OK.'

'And?'

'She told me to give you a message.'

I motioned for him to go on.

'To go round there some time. Go and see her.'

I nodded. 'Thanks.'

He looked at me with curiosity. 'Allora? Will you?'

'Yeah, maybe. Once this thing blows over.'

He looked at me for a second, like he was about to say something, but then turned back to the bees. They were still crawling up the ramp and into the hive. We watched them, both of us hypnotised by their busy industry.